Best Served Hot
Copyright©2015 Jimi Goninan
ISBN 978-1-909934-95-5
Cover art and design by Dawné Dominique

Published by
Lydian Press 2015
Find us on the World Wide Web at
www.lydianpress.com

Revenge has never been sweeter.

When Jameson loses everything he holds dear, he almost drowns in a sea of despair. Bitter and broken, he shuns his friends and retreats from the world. Then a chance encounter with a handsome young man offers him a glimmer of hope, and he slowly begins to piece his life back together. Will he be given the second chance at the love he so desperately deserves?

BEST SERVED HOT

Jimi Goninan

Lydian Press

To Nic,

Thank you for all your support, encouragement and friendship.

BEST SERVED HOT

Jameson's life was a mess – not the good, fun, quirky kind, mind you. Rather it was the kind of mess that had been heated up, left out in the rain and then put away at the back of the cupboard; mostly forgotten and gathering mold.

Three months had passed since his world had fallen apart and Jameson showed no signs of wanting to pick up the pieces and start the process of rebuilding. In fact, he seemed quite content to stay in his little cocoon, hiding from the world. In his defense, his life had exploded in such a spectacular fashion that it seemed he might have angered just about every deity known to man.

That hellish week had started off badly when the company he worked for had been subject to a hostile takeover. The new owners had a reputation for being ruthless in gutting their acquisitions and the following day he received confirmation that he was indeed now without gainful employment. This, in itself, hadn't all been so terrible, as he had a sizeable savings account and someone with his business acumen and head for numbers was quite employable. It just wasn't the best timing to say the least, as he was already a tad stressed, with his wedding to the love of his life, David, only two weeks away.

Two days later he'd received a rather odd phone call saying his final check to the caterers had bounced. It was only when he inquired at the bank that he learned he'd been the victim of credit card fraud...to the tune of several thousand dollars. Fortunately, his other bank account had remained untouched. However, the task of trying to sort the fraudulent purchases from the legitimate ones was complicated by all the miscellaneous wedding expenses they'd had over the past few months.

Again, Jameson had taken it in his stride but the next disaster proved to be a death knell for his resolve. Exactly one week before their nuptials, David, accompanied by Jameson's best friend since childhood – Judd – came to see him with something to confess.

"I'm sorry but I can't marry you," his fiancé began. "It's nothing you've done."

"We're in love," Judd had added.

And so the feeble explanations of their treacherous behavior continued while Jameson's heart simply shut down. He sat there, numbly, while they pleaded for forgiveness and understanding. Chances were he could have coped with any of the three traumas individually but with them all heaped together it was simply too overwhelming.

"Please leave," Jameson said, managing to keep his voice completely devoid of emotion.

The duplicitous duo had promptly left at which point Jameson's heart broke, as did his spirit. It was then that the crying started – and lasted off and on for about a month – followed by a bleak depression that saw Jameson retreat from his life completely. The one decent thing David managed to do was be the one who explained the situation to assorted family and friends – facing a good deal or wrath and scorn in the process. David also saw to the cancellation of all the wedding arrangements…it was the very least he could do, after all.

Jameson simply gave up. He spent his days self-medicating with alcohol and junk food, and losing himself in the comforting embrace of trashy television and porn. A nasty mixture of self-pity and misery kept Jameson wallowing in pain and saw him shun all attempts by his nearest and dearest to help pull him out of his cocoon of gloom. His parents even generously offered to pay for a holiday, so that Jameson could get away from Port Davinica for a while to help clear his head.

Jameson respectfully declined and stayed firmly ensconced at home instead.

After a while everyone decided to leave him be – bar the occasional call and text to make sure that he was still alive – and let him work through things in his own time.

Luckily, he lived in a beautiful, three-storey townhouse that he'd inherited from his paternal grandparents so he didn't need to worry about rent. Jameson also had regular food deliveries from the supermarket, so he didn't starve, but the closest thing to fruit or vegetables he consumed was the ready supply of wine. Money-wise his bank account still had a rather healthy balance, although it wouldn't sustain his slothful lifestyle indefinitely.

Trapped in a vicious cycle of regret and despair he berated himself, almost as much as those who'd wronged him, for his current predicament.

Why wasn't I enough? What did I do to deserve this? Did I nag him? Would he have left if my cock was bigger?

It would be fair to say that he wasn't in a healthy place mentally, or indeed physically. Jameson had been rather athletic but three months of little activity and an abysmal diet had taken its toll on his once fine form.

Things might have continued on in this destructive spiral if hadn't been for a slippery patch of white tiles on the bathroom floor. Jameson was stepping out the shower, following one of his increasingly infrequent self-washings, when his left foot suddenly slid from under him and he flailed desperately to right himself. His hands grasped for the towel rod by the door and in the process accidentally switched on the bright overhead light – he'd taken to showering in the dark. It was then that Jameson happened to catch sight of himself in the foggy mirror. There spread before him, through the light haze of steam, was a tired, pasty-looking and decidedly flabby man. Gone was his gym-honed body and in its place was a paunch with love handles thrown in for good measure. He didn't recognize himself. Granted, he was propped up by the towel rod at a thoroughly unflattering angle but Jameson recognized the reality of the situation.

Jameson had enabled the denial of his dire state by living in mostly darkness and avoiding reflective surfaces. The curtains were kept firmly shut and he chose to bathe himself in the soothing glow of his television instead. The shock was the wake up call he needed. In a flash he came to the first positive decision he had made in months.

No more!

Jameson knew that if he left it to tomorrow he wouldn't go so he quickly righted himself and dried off with a fluffy, red towel. Feeling energized by a sudden sense of steadfast purpose, he headed straight to his bedroom. Once there, Jameson began to frantically rifle through the mess of clothes on the floor.

When was the last time I did laundry?

Newly motivated, Jameson dressed in the baggiest clothes he could find – that were also reasonably clean – grabbed his keys and went straight out the front door for the first time in over a month. The air outside hit him like a refreshing wave as he bravely soldiered on to his car and then towards the first step of reclaiming his life – the gym.

* * *

"Welcome back!" said the fit-looking twink behind the counter at Sweat Station.

Despite the lad's friendly demeanor, Jameson had a sneaking suspicion that the twink was silently judging him for his wretched state.

Stop being so paranoid!

Jameson gave him a curt nod and a halfhearted smile before he determinedly continued on to the main weight and cardio section, where a faint, but not unpleasant, odor of masculine exertion hung in the air. When he saw his reflection in the multitude of mirrors, however, Jameson almost turned and fled. The harsh and unforgiving fluorescent glare showed how tired and unhealthy he was truly looking – apparently being cooped up and eating like a pig was not good for one's complexion. His skin looked ashen and blotchy, his hair was long and unkempt, and his eyes were bloodshot and glassy, and even in the loose clothing he could see himself bulging in all the wrong places.

His previous muscular bulk had seemingly migrated and set up camp around his middle.

What have I done to myself?

The man staring back from the mirror looked far older than Jameson's twenty-five years. Luckily, the gym was practically deserted due to the late hour. He didn't know what he would have done if he'd seen somebody he knew. All the posters depicting ripped models advertising CocKed underwear, adorning the gym walls, didn't help his state of mind – particularly the lad with the tousled black hair, china blue eyes and full lips…exactly his type.

To well and truly establish the extent of his decline, Jameson went to the electronic scales located at the side of the cardio area to weigh himself. He stood there looking at the scales for a good two minutes before he worked up the courage to actually step on the plate.

Do it! It's just like ripping off a Band-Aid! Man up!

Jameson took a deep breath and stepped forward. The number that appeared on the green glowing display nearly sent him into a fit of tears. Not only had he lost his musculature but he'd also gained a whopping ten kilos of pure fat. Jameson stared at the display in disbelief. His mind whirled, part of him wanted to flee and pretend everything was fine while another part protested strongly that he rectify the situation post haste. Jameson battled with himself for what seemed an eternity but eventually the side calling for immediate action won out. Deep down he knew that he had to start living again and the only way to do that was to face his problems head on.

Jameson had always been very sporty, ever since he was a child, and had consequently never struggled with body issues. This only served to make his current predicament all the more distressing, as he didn't know how to deal with his feelings of embarrassment and shame.

Once the voice of denial was properly silenced – for the time being at least – Jameson took himself to the nearest treadmill and hopped on. Despite his desperate situation, he was sensible and didn't go full blast into his old routine, as he couldn't even begin to imagine how much speed and stamina he had lost to his hibernation and he didn't want to run the risk of injuring himself.

Jameson entered a light program and pressed the big green START button. After only five minutes he was puffing and panting, but it only served to solidify his resolve. By the time the announcement came over the PA system warning of the impending closing time he was dripping with sweat and thoroughly exhausted. He finished up, wiped the equipment down and then proceeded directly home to shower – there was no way he would be showering at the gym in his current condition. Jameson was too mortified by what he had become to risk inflicting his naked form on anyone else.

As he drove home Jameson vowed that he would get back to his former healthy state no matter how much time it took.

"It better not take too damn long," he mumbled to himself, as the image of the electronic display flashed back through his troubled mind.

* * *

Upon returning home, Jameson opened the front door and was confronted by the almost overwhelming rank smell of his townhouse.

Did something die in here?

In that moment he realized that it had – namely his hope and dignity….as well as the remains of quite a few fast food deliveries. Jameson knew that circumstances had conspired against him but it was he who had refused all offers of help and chosen to wallow instead.

Jameson closed the door behind him and headed upstairs to take a nice long hot shower, with the lights on – no more hiding. He let the soothing hot water wash away the traces of his exertion and revive his tired body. Once done, he toweled off and made his back to his bedroom to ready himself for the next task. Squished down at the back of the cupboard, Jameson managed to find some more clean clothes. They were snug, not to mention desperately out of fashion, but would do the job.

First, he attacked the kitchen, opening all the cupboards and putting all of his comfort food into plastic bags, which he placed by the front door in a neat pile. Jameson planned to drop them at a homeless shelter the following day. Then he went through the townhouse rounded up all his dirty clothes and dumped them in the laundry to begin the first of many loads. As the washing machine went about its work, with a low rumble, so did Jameson. He began the arduous task of cleaning the townhouse from top to bottom, figuring his home needed a fresh start as much as his body did.

Jameson threw open all of the curtains and windows to really air out the place, not caring if the neighbors could see in...although given the time it was doubtful they'd still be awake. Fortunately, it was a rather mild night with a touch of spring in the air and the fragrant scent of fresh flowers soon washed through the place to replace the staleness.

He moved from room to room bagging up all the trash and generally tidying up. Jameson was slightly disturbed by the amount of empty wine bottles he found about the place. He resolved to steer clear of alcohol, as well as all the sweet and savory treats he'd been consuming, while he was back on the health bandwagon.

The cleaning was going great guns until he pulled out a dark red tie that belonged to David from under the bed in the master bedroom. Jameson stayed there on his knees, stuck in place, just staring the piece of material in his hand. It had been one of the ties he'd hated, but the feelings of loss and betrayal all came flooding back and a wave of emotion threatened to drown him in despair once more. Tears started to roll down his face and he might very well have stayed there the whole night had he not heard the alarm sounding the end of his latest load of laundry.

Jameson's steely resolve came back and he climbed up to the attic and grabbed an old cardboard box. He then spent the next hour scouring the townhouse for every last trace of his ex-fiancé. David hadn't left much there but each new find saw Jameson's heart hardened even more. Once he had everything in a box he threw it into the fireplace, struck a match and watched with a triumphant grin as the glorious fire consumed the remnants of his past. Jameson felt cleansed and filled with a very satisfying inner glow.

The scorned soul then continued about his work until the townhouse was practically spotless. Jameson glanced at the grandfather clock in the hall on his way up to bed and saw that it was nearly 5am. It had been time consuming but well worth the effort. Jameson climbed into bed feeling better than he had in months and soon drifted off into a most contented, and wonderfully deep, sleep.

* * *

The first thing Jameson did, when he awoke from his restful slumber the following afternoon, was to ring his usual beauty salon ‑ A Close Shave – to see if they could book him in that day for a deluxe package. He had neglected his regular regime long enough and thought that he more than deserved a little pampering after all that activity the previous night. Fortunately, they had just had two cancellations and could fit in him, but only if he came straight away. He quickly put on what he had hoped to be a rather slimming outfit of jeans and a tailored navy-blue jacket, which helped but couldn't completely disguise his fall from grace. The salon was only three blocks away so he didn't have far to go.

On the way Jameson suddenly realized he was starving, as he hadn't had time to have breakfast. His body was desperately craving sugar and caffeine, so he stopped by a nearby café, on the way, to grab a coffee and low-fat bran muffin to tide him over. While not as nutritious a meal as he should be having, it was a far sight better than his usual breakfast of leftover pizza and donuts.

The barista greeted him with a dazzling white smile that made Jameson's heart flutter just a little and his mind wander to a less than polite place. It was the first non-porn related arousal he'd experienced in months and it gave him hope that he was indeed back on the right track.

Mmm…tasty.

Jameson smiled in return but then was hit by an instant wave of self-doubt.

He's just being friendly. You're still a mess, stop deluding yourself!

Yet Jameson couldn't quite shake the feeling of familiarity from the beautiful barista, but it was more likely that the man's raven black hair and alabaster skin reminded him of his ex-fiancé – it was a look he'd always been drawn to.

He'd only end up hurting you like David! Do you really want to spend months nursing another heartbreak?

The renewed thought of the painful breakup left Jameson unsettled and quite a bit less bouncy than he'd left the house. He paid for his order and continued on to his appointment.

"Have a wonderful day," said the barista to Jameson's rapidly fleeing form.

By the time he reached the salon his mood had sunk even further. His ego was then dealt another blow when Cameron, the manager of the salon, greeted him with an "Oh dear!"

This only served to confirm his worst fears. In his defense, Cameron had never seen Jameson in such a sorry state.

"Not to worry, we'll soon have you back to your former glory," Cameron assured Jameson, after seeing the distraught look on his client's face. Jameson would have been offended if he didn't happen to fully agree with Cameron's assessment of his current appearance.

First, Cameron guided him into cubicle at the end of the hallway to begin his treatments. Cameron, along with his new apprentice Nora – the mani/pedi/brow/facial combo called for two people – set to work buffing, filing, plucking, soaking and doing their very best to coax Jameson's face and nails back to their sparkling best.

An hour later Jameson emerged from the cubicle, his face tingling and his self-confidence very much on the mend. Granted, he knew that he had to put in a lot more work at the gym to get his health and body back to where they were before his misfortune began but these little cosmetic changes were the baby steps he needed to begin the long road to recovery – both physically and mentally.

Cameron then placed Jameson in the big black padded chair facing the mirror and into the capable hands of Javier – a swarthy gent of Cuban descent and their resident hair stylist.

"I need something completely new," said Jameson, determined to recapture his former confidence.

"Leave it to me, honey," replied Javier, sassy as ever.

The hairdresser fussed over the unkempt mess before him for a few moments before, with a flash of inspiration in his eyes, he apparently came to a decision. He soon set to work applying foils to add a splash of color to Jameson's lackluster locks and popped him under the dryer to accelerate the process. While they were waiting for the chemicals to do their work Nora brought Jameson a soothing cup of green tea and some trashy magazines to read.

The time passed quickly and soon Jameson's head was tilted back as Javier strong hands rinsed out the product and gave his scalp a thorough massage. The pleasantly warm water and the hairdresser's strong fingers felt absolutely divine. Jameson always found this part of the hairdressing experience quasi-erotic – especially when looking up into Javier's soulful black eyes.

Before too long, Javier's skilled hands and trusty silver scissors had transformed the scruffy mop on top of Jameson's head into a much more fashionable style. Jameson was delighted with the result and felt like a brand new man...although he wasn't going to get one until his body was in better shape. For some reason the image of the barista sauntered back into his mind. Jameson didn't know why the young man had made such an impression on him but this time he was less hasty to dismiss his wanton thoughts and allowed himself to linger in the fantasy just a little bit longer.

With his self esteem much improved he happily paid the hefty – yet completely justified – bill and bid adieu to his trusted beauty therapists.

It was amazing how much better he felt, almost like he was slipping out of his crusty shell and back into the Jameson he used to know. He practically skipped back to the townhouse. On the way back home Jameson swung by the grocery store to stock up on fruit, vegetables and everything else healthy that he'd been avoiding for the last few months.

Once home again, his groceries all put away, Jameson looked about the townhouse and realized that the simple clean up he'd done the previous evening wasn't going to be enough. His home needed a makeover as much as he did. Jameson was determined to have a fresh start, and eradicate the memories of the man he'd lived with for two years. The man who'd betrayed him. The man who'd crushed his heart.

The man I still love.

Jameson could feel fresh tears building and decided the best course of action was to keep himself busy, so he spent the rest of the day rearranging just about every room in the house. Several sweaty hours later, the vibe of the place felt far more positive and full of possibility. Whether it was the Feng Shui or just his imagination Jameson didn't know or particularly care. He was content to be moving on with his life.

He rested for thirty minutes or so and then toddled off to the gym again, determined to keep on moving with his plan of recovery. Jameson chose to do only cardio, figuring that moving all the furniture about had been enough of a weights workout. After thirty minutes on the treadmill, Jameson was happy to discover that his body made it through another session without too much complaint.

Maybe I'm not so far gone, after all.

2

Over the next few days Jameson developed something of the routine. He started each morning with a healthy breakfast – usually an egg white, mushroom and tomato omelet coupled with some fruit – followed by pottering about the house or out in the garden replanting the numerous flowerbeds. In the afternoons he took himself off to the café with the handsome barista – Perk Up – to read quietly for a few hours, while enjoying a soothing pot of Earl Grey tea. He was still unemployed – not having had the energy or inclination to search for a new position – so he certainly had the time. Then he'd return home for a light dinner before he headed off to Sweat Station for his daily workout.

Even though he was starting to feel much better about his prospects, Jameson was still going to the gym late at night to avoid running into anyone he knew. It wasn't just the thought of them noticing his less than buff state – although that was certainly a consideration – it was more the looks of pity he feared. The broken engagement and affair was well known in his social circles and he just couldn't face the inevitable condolences and rehashing of the whole saga…not yet.

Not to say that he was content to be a loner the rest of his days. It was just that he needed a little more time before diving back into his previously extremely sociable lifestyle. Jameson knew that he would have to deal with these social interactions eventually, so he made a few calls and texts, arranging catch-ups for the following month, which gave him a respite of four weeks. He would just have to do his best to grin and swallow down the pain – instead of screaming like a banshee – whenever anyone asked how he was feeling.

The afternoons soon became his favorite part of the day. Perk Up was located at the base of Graywood Gardens – an apartment complex full to bursting with gentlemen of a certain persuasion – as well as facing the pleasing landscape of Janeway Park. The big glass walls at the front of the café provided patrons with wonderful views of the all the trees and flowers of the park, as well as the comings and goings of the shapely tenants of the building. Jameson soon had a favorite spot, tucked away in the corner of the café, and with a wonderfully comfortable overstuffed brown leather armchair and a small table. It provided him with a modicum of privacy while still letting him gaze lazily at the goings on outside the window.

The café always had a pleasing aroma of freshly made coffee mingled together with the tempting scent of pastries. Every day the barista welcomed him with a winning smile that always made Jameson's day a little bit brighter and he found that he couldn't help but give a wide, friendly smile in return. Jameson could see by his nametag that the lad's name was 'Nicolas' but their conversation still hadn't gone further than his order and generic comments about the weather. If the situation had been different Jameson would have flirted and tried to get his number by now but he still felt far too damaged for anything new in his life…no matter how alluring he found Nicolas' full red lips and china blue eyes.

On the fourth day things took an unexpected turn when Nicolas approached Jameson after the latter had been there for about an hour. They were the only two souls in the café.

"You know your eyes are amazing," remarked the barista.

The sound of the smooth baritone voice always gave Jameson a light tingling feeling in his stomach.

"Thank you," said Jameson, smiling shyly.

"But you must get told that all time," Nicolas added.

"Not as often as I'd like," joked Jameson.

It was true that people often remarked favorably upon his eyes. They were unusual in that they were heterochromatic – one a warm amber and the other a crystal blue. Jameson liked that this quirk of genetics made him stand out.

"So, now that I've buttered you up, how'd you like to be my guinea pig?" asked Nicolas, a cheeky grin upon his face.

"Ummm..." said Jameson, completely thrown by the question.

"I'm working on a new signature coffee for the café," Nicolas hastened to add upon seeing the look of confusion on his customer's face.

"Sure, why not."

Admittedly, Jameson was flattered by the attention that Nicolas was showing him, but he didn't want to read anything into it.

"What's your name, by the way? I mean I should know who I've killed if it all goes horribly wrong," joked the comely coffee maker.

"Jameson James."

Why did I just give my full name? Who does that?

"Nicolas Nightingale. Pleased to meet you."

The barista gave Jameson's hand a firm, friendly shake. Jameson smiled, both from the contact and amused by the alliteration of their names. He was reluctant to let go of Nicolas' hand but also didn't want to make things awkward.

"You too."

Jameson could feel the warmth sweeping up his face, powerless to stop it, as he blushed like an embarrassed schoolboy. He desperately hoped that Nicolas hadn't noticed.

"So, I have a few different concoctions I'm been experimenting with. I won't tell you what they are until afterwards. We should be scientific and unbiased after all," said Nicolas, a look of mock seriousness on his face.

"Of course."

Jameson felt himself warming to Nicolas even more. Nicolas went back behind the counter and busily set about preparing the drinks for Jameson to try. For his part, Jameson was enjoying himself. He hadn't realized just how much he missed human company.

A few minutes later Nicolas returned with the beverages and set them before Jameson. He was glad the barista had only made a mini-version of each, as he knew he'd been bouncing off the walls if he had three full-strength coffees inside him.

The first was sickly-sweet, with an almost overpowering combination of vanilla, butterscotch and honey. Jameson was something of a sweet tooth but even he found it far too sugary. The second was more bitter – especially after the sweetness of the first – and Jameson had to restrain himself from spitting it straight back out again. Out of politeness he finished it and had to concede that he did like the almond aftertaste when he was done. The third and final concoction proved to be the winner finding a nice balance between the bitterness of the coffee and the sugary additives. The taste was familiar to Jameson but he couldn't quite place it.

"The last one," Jameson announced when he'd finished his impromptu tasting session.

"Yeah, that's my favorite too, but I thought it best to get a few independent opinions."

"So, what's the name of your creation?" asked Jameson with genuine interest.

"The Speculatté! Thanks for your help."

"My pleasure. Aren't you going to tell me what's in it?"

"Well I could, but you know what they say…"

"You'd have to kill me?" asked Jameson, anticipating the old joke.

"No, I have far better ways to keep boys from talking."

"Well, it is hard to speak with your mouth full."

Jameson was a little taken aback at his own brazenness.

"You know it!!"

And with that the barista moved off to go about his chores in preparation for the after-work crowd. Jameson blushed again and watched him go with a tinge of regret and confusion.

Why are you flirting like a two-dollar truck stop whore? But he's so cute! You're not ready. It's only a bit of fun. Did you forget that you're pretty much an emotional basket case?

The inner turmoil continued on for a good half hour, during which time Jameson did his very best not to blatantly stare at Nicolas. Eventually, he tired of the competing voices and decided to clear his head by heading home. Jameson gave Nicolas the briefest of goodbyes and exited the café before his resolve to leave faltered.

Fifteen minutes later, Jameson closed the front door of the terrace behind him and sunk down to the floor.

If only I wasn't such a mess.

* * *

By the end of the week Jameson was no longer taking the car, but instead walking the two kilometers, to and from the gym. He felt his old energy and enthusiasm for life slowly returning.

Despite his decision to avoid contact with friends for another month, there was someone who he knew that he had to see – Ruby. One of his oldest and dearest friends, she was a striking redhead, with cool blue eyes, dangerous curves and was a private detective to boot – all in all, one hell of a package. They had been firm friends since college and had seen each other through all sorts of shenanigans…such as that time in the hot tub with those strapping Swedish twins; who were identical in all but their proclivities.

Ruby had consistently messaged him throughout his self-imposed exile, regardless of his apathy in responding. She had given him space but was now starting to become impatient, especially when she found out that Jameson had been leaving the house again. Mrs Mears, a dear old thing and one of Jameson's elderly neighbors, had been friends with Ruby's late grandmother and had known the detective since she was a toddler. When Jameson had locked himself away, Ruby had asked the housebound lady to keep an eye out for him…not a particularly big imposition seeing she spent most of her time gazing out at the street and the activities of her neighbors.

So upon hearing of the hermit's return to the outside world she began to message and call daily until Jameson finally agreed to meet with her. And so, here they were, sitting in Jameson's garden, under the shade of the two small oak trees, enjoying iced tea and chatting pleasantly.

Ruby had tactfully not brought up Jameson's appearance, something, which he was very grateful for.

"I'm glad you're back in the land of the living," said the vivacious redhead.

"Yeah. I just needed some space but I don't think I really did myself any favors."

"Clearly." Ruby was nothing if not forthright. "Although, now that you've finished wallowing, we need to get you back to the lovable lad you were before this all nasty business."

"Well, I'm back at the gym."

"Fantastic."

"And…" Jameson was a tad reluctant to reveal the extent of his house cleansing but thought if anyone would understand it would be Ruby, "…and I burnt all the stuff he left behind."

"Good boy! Personally, I would've waited until those bastards were standing in the middle of it before throwing in the match!"

Ruby let out a delightfully wicked laugh. Jameson was feeling much better and regretted not meeting up with Ruby sooner.

"So what about work? Are you going to go back to finance?" inquired Ruby.

"I honestly don't know."

"What about your writing? I loved all those short stories you did at college."

"Well I haven't really done anything for ages. Besides, it's hardly the most stable of professions."

"You sound like your father!"

"Yeah, yeah, I know. I'll think about it."

Apparently satisfied by her efforts Ruby moved onto the next pressing issue.

"Now what about sex? Porn isn't going to last you forever."

Jameson's face flushed. He was used to the bawdy side of his friend, but he felt it was all a bit too soon for such talk

.

"You need to climb right back on the horse...or any horse-like thing you can find," she continued with a cheeky grin.

They both laughed, although Jameson knew he wasn't ready for a casual fling.

Not yet...although there is a certain barista who'd certainly fit the bill.

They passed the rest of the afternoon in agreeable companionship and made plans to catch up for coffee later the following week.

* * *

Over the next month Jameson went hard at the gym and managed to banish nearly all of his depressed excess. While the first seven kilos seemed to fly off the last three were a little more stubborn but he persevered and eventually his metabolism began to return to its former high levels rather than the sluggish low they had sunk to.

His skin also showed the benefits of his improved fitness; he'd lost that pale, greasy pallor and was the very picture of health. Indeed, he was looking far better than he had in quite some time.

Jameson stuck to his much-improved eating plan, for the most part, although it wasn't all plain sailing. His impulse to devour something cream-filled and sugary, when maudlin thoughts would cross his mind, was awfully compelling but he stayed strong and the urges began to lessen as the weeks wore on.

In his drive to shake off his malaise and move forward again, Jameson had updated his resume and sent it off to a variety of recruitment agencies in the hopes of finding gainful employment. Even though he hadn't any enticing offers so far, he was quietly confident that it was only a matter of time before he found what he was looking for.

In the meantime, Jameson had taken Ruby's suggestion to heart and had unearthed his stash of stories that had been silently languishing away up in the attic, along with all his mementos from college. He was still spending most afternoons at Perk Up, reading, writing and generally trying to reinvigorate his creative juices. More and more, Jameson felt that he was coming back to himself.

The change in his character was apparent to everyone, Nicolas included. Their friendship had grown over the weeks and Jameson had come discover quite a lot about the young barista, such as the fact that he was Canadian, and was actually the manager of the café despite only being twenty-one years old. The other important tidbit Jameson had gleaned was that Nicolas was single, which had become increasingly obvious as their light-hearted conversations became gradually filled with more and more flirting.

"Come on, spoil yourself have the caramel cheesecake," said the barista, in a rather convincing manner.

"No, I'm being good," protested Jameson with a smile.

"You can afford it, you're looking really fit," countered the cheeky barista.

Jameson gave into peer pressure and had to admit, after he'd practically inhaled the dessert, that it was delicious.

As much as he enjoyed his time with Nicolas, Jameson couldn't help but feel that he was nowhere near ready for a new relationship. In spite of this, Jameson still had a nagging sense that he had known the barista before he'd started coming to the café but assumed he must be mistaken. That was until that is Nicolas squatted to pick up a napkin off the floor and his blue jeans slipped downwards to reveal the waistband of his CocKed underwear. In a flash it came to him with a blinding clarity.

"You're a CocKed boy!" he blurted out, much to the amusement of the two elderly ladies by the door who'd been enjoying a quiet cup of tea.

Nicolas turned around with a sheepish smile.

"Yeah, I usually don't get recognized with my clothes on."

The barista gave Jameson a mischievous wink, before heading back behind the counter. Jameson couldn't believe it had taken him so long to realize that his friendly barista was the very same man he'd seen plastered all over the walls of his gym. He'd certainly looked longingly enough at the posters while he was training. After that, Jameson found it practically impossible to concentrate on anything but the thought of Nicolas lazing about in his underwear beckoning him closer.

Half an hour later, after he had read the same page for the tenth time, Jameson admitted defeat and packed up his belongings. As he was paying for his tea and cake the voices in his head were locked in a ferocious battle.

Ask him out! No, you're not ready! What's the worst that can happen? Crushing disappointment!

"Nicolas…"

"Yeah?"

"I just…I just wanted to…"

Jameson could see a look of curiosity on Nicolas' face but just couldn't bring himself to take the next step.

"...to say congrats on the modeling."

Chicken!

"You look great!" added Jameson.

"Thanks! I always appreciate a compliment from a handsome man."

The barista's interest couldn't have been more blatant if he'd hopped over the counter and began to wildly make love to Jameson right there and then on the floor of the café.

He wants you! I can't! Why the hell not? It's too much, too soon and I can't be hurt like that again.

"See you later," said Jameson, edging away from the counter.

"Look forward to it."

Jameson could plainly see the warmth in Nicolas' eyes, but he felt embarrassed, flustered and confused. He practically fled out the door, all the while silently berating himself for his cowardice.

* * *

After pondering over his dwindling savings once again, Jameson decided that he needed to do something to earn some extra money until he found a new job. The solution came to him as he was rearranging some boxes down in the basement. Many years beforehand his grandparents had converted the basement into a studio apartment, with a separate entrance, for when their adult grandchildren had come to stay, as they'd wanted to give them their privacy. Jameson had lived there for a year or so while he had finished his studies but it hadn't been used for anything but storage in a long while. Jameson spent an afternoon moving all the various boxes and accumulated junk up to the attic and then made sure that all the plumbing and electricity was still in good working order. Once he had the place fresh and clean Jameson placed ads on various accommodation websites.

Jameson didn't think he'd have any trouble finding tenants as his was a desirable neighborhood – smack bang in the middle of Port Davinica's main gayborhood – close to the biggest park in the city and with easy access to public transport. Jameson was soon proved correct when his inbox was inundated with inquiries the following day. He whittled them down to around twenty possible applicants and set up appointments for them to come and look over the apartment.

A few days later Jameson was beginning to lose hope that he'd ever find a suitable tenant. He'd had about ten no-shows, which he found unspeakably rude and the ones that did turn up seemed to show far more interest in him than the apartment...flattering but hardly what he was looking for. Jameson was waiting on one last guy before he headed off to the gym but wasn't feeling particularly hopeful. At the appointed time there was a knock on the front door and Jameson opened it to find a cute young man, with spiky black hair, friendly brown eyes and a cheeky smile.

"Hi, I'm Matt," said the stranger.

"Jameson. Nice to meet you."

"You too."

They shook hands and Jameson began the tour of the apartment. The duo clicked straight away, chatting all the while Jameson showed him around. Jameson discovered that Matt was studying to become a marine biologist at the local University whilst working part-time at The Grand Babylon Hotel. Matt was looking for somewhere cheap and central, and appeared to love the apartment.

By the time Jameson had finished showing Matt the apartment and the leafy backyard he'd decided that he definitely wanted the bubbly, young man as a tenant.

"So what do you think?" asked Jameson, hoping for a positive reply.

"When can I move in?" said an enthusiastic Matt in return.

"As soon as you like."

His new tenant moved in the following weekend, helped by his equally cute boyfriend Trent…a tall lad with cropped black hair, ice blue eyes and a lean, defined build. The couple had been co-workers, and friends, for the last three years but had only recently gotten together. Consequently, they were very much in the honeymooner stage of their relationship and were practically glued at the hip with constant displays of affection.

Over the next few weeks Jameson saw quite a lot of the lads and found he enjoyed their company. Initially, Jameson wasn't sure that he could handle regularly seeing so much loving adoration. Fortunately, Jameson warmed to Trent as quickly as he had to Matt and soon found the open affection between the pair sweet and quite adorable, even if it was also a painful reminder of what he had lost from his own life.

The trio ate together regularly on the terrace – breakfasts and dinners – and their companionship made him feel far less lonely rattling around the big townhouse all by himself. Not that he was ready for another live-in lover by any means, although he still enjoyed the occasional daydream of being happily coupled once more…usually with Nicolas playing the role of the doting boyfriend.

If only I wasn't such a scaredy-cat.

* * *

In the meantime, Jameson still hadn't had any success finding another job. Not that he hadn't had offers but he just wasn't feeling inspired by any of them. He was considering a complete change of career. As a child he had had two loves – writing and numbers. Both of which Jameson had excelled in, consistently receiving top marks in both mathematics and English all throughout his schooling. His father, however, had hammered into Jameson the importance of having a stable career behind him, so he'd ended up pursuing a career in the much safer world of accounting.

Jameson had enjoyed his work at first but, to be honest, it hadn't been fulfilling for quite some time. That being said, Jameson was realistic and knew that a creative career could set him up for a life of rejection and financial disappointment.

It was then that life through him another curve ball, as it is want to do, when he received a most unexpected and curious offer from Ruby. She had been working on a case to help catch an adulterous spouse. Usually, she would perform the 'honey trap' herself to help expose the philandering partner, but unfortunately in this instance she lacked the proper equipment – namely male genitalia. As compensation for his troubles, Ruby offered to pay Jameson half her fee.

"All you'd have to do is try and pick him up at the bar and I'll take care of the rest," Ruby reassured Jameson.

At first, Jameson was hesitant. It wasn't something that he'd ever dreamed of doing, but the more he thought about it, the more the idea of outing a cheater appealed to him.

If only someone had done that for me. Besides, it's hardly like I'd be in any danger and the money would come in handy.

Jameson rang Ruby the following morning and together they set up the sting for that Friday night. As the day came closer Jameson found his nervousness give way to a darker feeling, one of righteous vengeance…he liked how it felt.

Finally, the day arrived and Jameson was filled with excitement. He felt like a spy on a secret mission. Granted, he wasn't about to foil a plot for world domination but if he could make life utterly miserable for one unfaithful man he'd be happy. As Jameson dressed in his favorite, impeccably tailored, navy-blue suit – a perfect fit after his gym work – his excitement was tempered with a twinge of sadness as the last time he'd worn it was for his and David's engagement party. The reminder of the betrayal hardened his heart once more and put him in the ideal frame of mind for the task at hand.

Thirty minutes later, Jameson arrived at the target's favorite hunting ground – the cocktail bar of The Grand Babylon Hotel – and took a seat at the bar. Fortunately, Matt and Trent weren't working that evening so he was in no danger of running into his tenants and possibly giving the game away. The bar was quite up-market; the minimalist décor was in keeping with the tasteful elegance of rest of the hotel. The formal dress code added a certain touch of class, as the bar was only populated with men in expensive suits and women in evening dresses.

Jameson had studied the photo of the client's husband that Ruby had given him, so knew his prey by sight, and soon spotted him sitting only a few stools away. A strikingly handsome man with cropped blond hair and sea-green eyes. He wasn't sure how to begin but fortune lent Jameson a hand and the gent in question looked his way and smiled. His natural reaction was to smile then look away in a display of shyness, which turned out to be rather endearing and apparently exactly what the guy needed to come over and introduce himself.

"Hi, I'm Marcus."

His sharp, black suit highlighted the muscular form beneath, which caused Jameson's crotch to swell ever so slightly.

"Christopher," replied Jameson. Ruby had instructed him to use a false name.

"Drink?" offered Marcus.

"Sure. I'll have a Mojito Royale, thanks."

"Sounds good. I think I'll have the same."

After Marcus ordered the drinks, the two fell into easy conversation. Jameson had been worried that he'd be out of practice flirting – he hadn't dated anyone new in over three years – but it turned out he was a natural. Soon the conversation turned more intimate and Jameson relaxed into the role, buoyed by the fact that an attractive man was showing interest in him. One drink followed another and before he knew it Jameson was feeling rather tipsy. Their legs had been rubbing up against one another for the past fifteen minutes and there was a growing sexual tension between the pair.

"So, I've got a room here at the hotel if you'd like to come upstairs for a while?" asked Marcus suggestively.

Jameson was caught up in the moment and eagerly agreed. When they stepped into the empty elevator Marcus pushed Jameson up against the wall and kissed him deeply. Jameson responded in kind, his body desperately craving the touch of another man. Lust flooded through Jameson's body and brain. He could feel Marcus' impressive erection pressed up against his own. Jameson hadn't been with anyone since David and he was ready to explode.

They soon arrived on Marcus' floor and the traitorous spouse took Jameson's hand and led him to the room. Once inside they resumed their passionate kissing. It hadn't been part of the plan to actually sleep with the target but Jameson was only thinking with one head and it wasn't the one known for its good judgment.

Thankfully he was saved from making a most unwise decision. Marcus broke away from the kiss and led Jameson further into the room.

"Make yourself comfortable, handsome. I'll be back in a sec," said Marcus, as he disappeared into the bathroom.

The object of temptation now removed, Jameson was able to regain his senses and quickly fled the room and hightailed it back to Ruby's car in the garage under the hotel, all the while hoping Ruby had what she needed.

Jameson waited nervously by the detective's red two-door BMW convertible – a gift from a grateful former client. His heart was racing as he paced up and down, anxious that Marcus may come looking for him. When Ruby arrived a few minutes later, a wave of relief surged through Jameson.

"You OK," asked Ruby, upon noticing Jameson's flushed face and nervous disposition.

"Yeah, I think so. Did you get it?"

Jameson was more than eager to know the results of their operation.

"Yes, I'll show you later. First, we better get out of here before your playmate works out what we've done and decides to come find you."

Ruby started the car and soon sped out of the car park, headed back to Jameson's townhouse.

Before too long they were comfortably installed in the lounge room enjoying a big pot of Earl Grey tea – mainly to help settle Jameson's nerves. Between them sat Ruby's laptop, its screen full of compromising pictures of Marcus and Jameson in the bar and from the elevator. Ruby was friendly with the head of security of the hotel and had easily obtained the footage from the hotel's security cameras, with the promise of a bottle of fine Scotch.

Jameson was on a bit of a high after the experience and while it didn't take all the pain away from his own betrayal he did feel a bit better. The two friends continued to chat amiably for about an hour before Ruby had to leave.

"Time to go break the unhappy news," said Ruby, obviously not looking forward to the chore ahead. "Thanks again for today, you were wonderful,"

"It was fun. I'd happily do it again."

"Well, there may actually be something else you can help me with. I have to do a bit more background research but I'll keep you posted."

"Great!"

Maybe I've found my new calling.

After Ruby had left, Jameson made his way upstairs to his bedroom and stripped down to his underwear. He was still riled up by the encounter with Marcus and needed to find his release. Driven by lust he went online and downloaded the latest offering from New Sodom Productions, featuring his favorite stars – Cody Fox and Brady Summers. Their scenes were always guaranteed to be sizzling, as the duo had incredible chemistry. Cody was a cute brunette with hazel eyes and a lean, twinkish build, which seemed almost too small for the monster meat he packed between his legs – eleven inches in total – honestly, the thing looked like another limb. Brady, on the other hand, while still having a sizeable appendage – part of the job description really – was much more muscular with surfer-like blond hair and a tanned bubble butt that just begged to be plowed...which Cody often did. Jameson had been delighted, and even more turned on, when he discovered that they were now a real-life couple, a fact made even hotter given that Brady had apparently been a happily married heterosexual beforehand. Who hasn't harbored a secret desire to turn a straight boy?

Jameson pulled down his briefs and took his rock-hard erection in hand. It only took a few minutes of watching the sweaty shenanigans of his fantasy playmates onscreen before his body tensed up as he ejaculated. His thick white seed spurted up into the air and splattered back down over his defined chest, before it leaked down over his recently recovered abs. Jameson decided to clean up in the shower and headed to the bathroom, careful not to drip any cum onto the floor – he didn't want any unsightly stains on the carpeting, after all.

As the hot water washed away the traces of his sin, Jameson's mind started to wander. The release had felt good, but once the bliss of the orgasm began to fade his thoughts turned back to his actions that night and the betrayal involved. Naturally, this soon led him back to his own cuckolding at the hands of his fiancé and best friend, where he had lost his partner and his most trusted confidant all in one fell swoop.

David and he had been so happy – or so Jameson had thought. As much as he hated both of them, he still strangely missed their presence in his life. Part of him wished things could go back to how they were before he discovered the truth, but in his heart he knew that their perfect, happy life had been nothing but a fantasy.

It seemed bizarre that David had run off with Judd, given they had hated each other at first. Indeed, they had allegedly only tolerated each other through their mutual devotion to Jameson.

Even now, Jameson didn't know which was the worse act of disloyalty – that of David or Judd. The latter had been his best friend since their first day of school and had always been there for one another. Granted, Jameson knew well Judd's reputation of wreaking havoc on relationships – his own and others – treating men as little more than a handy outlet for his libido. That being said, he never dreamed that Judd would sacrifice their friendship in his seemingly never-ending pursuit of cock. Jameson refused to believe that the duplicitous duo could possibly be in love…he was fairly sure they were heartless.

They had repeatedly tried contacting him since that ill-fated day when they had stood before him and confessed their sins, both proclaiming not to want to hurt him but not being able to help how they felt. Jameson didn't think he could ever forgive them and had no intention of ever allowing them back into his life.

In hindsight, he was a fool for not seeing the affair. The late nights at the office, the lessening of their sex life…but he'd stayed blissfully ignorant and it had come back to smack him firmly in the ass – something he ordinarily wouldn't have minded.

Jameson couldn't help but wonder if he had driven David away. In his darker moments, like now, he let in all sorts of crushing negativity and self-doubt.

Was I not supportive enough? Did I not understand his needs? Am I rubbish in bed? Was it really my fault after all?

* * *

The following afternoon Jameson went to the café, as usual, but wasn't feeling quite himself. He'd spent most of the past night tossing and turning, dwelling on the failure of his relationship and the betrayal he still felt. Not to mention questioning the motives of the male species in general.

"You, OK? You seem a little down," inquired Nicolas gently.

"No, I'm fine," Jameson replied a little more gruffly than he'd intended.

The smile on Nicolas' face faltered slightly and he went back about his business, cleaning behind the counter.

Why are you pushing him away?

Jameson took his order and went to his spot to sulk. He knew he should stop feeling sorry for himself, but he couldn't shake the thought that he'd never be able to trust anyone enough to find love again. He barely stayed half an hour before he packed up waved a brief goodbye to Nicolas and hurried home. When he got there he quickly dumped his bag in the study, climbed the stairs, undressed and turned on the shower. Jameson then sat down on shower floor and had a good, long cry. The pressure of the hot water comforted him as he sobbed and let his emotions run riot.

After twenty minutes – thank goodness for endless hot water systems – Jameson emerged from his steamy cocoon feeling much better. He dried off and wrapped himself up in a soft, fluffy, over-sized towel before heading to the bedroom. Feeling more than a little lovelorn, Jameson climbed into bed, tired after his emotional outpouring; he soon felt the embrace of slumber overtaking him. There was, however, one little thought that made its way into his mind before he drifted off completely.

Perhaps I need to see a therapist?

* * *

Jameson hadn't been to the café in over two weeks, feeling ashamed of how he'd treated Nicolas the last time. He needn't have worried, for as soon as he entered the café Jameson was greeted by Nicolas' dazzling, warm smile.

"There you are, handsome! I thought you'd abandoned me for another barista," joked Nicolas.

"Never! Sorry, for being such a grump last time."

Jameson was eager to make amends and relieved that Nicolas didn't appear to be harboring a grudge.

"It's fine. We all have our off days, but don't make it a habit or I'll have to give you a jolly good spanking. Speculatté?"

"Yes please," answered Jameson, although it wasn't clear whether that was in response to the coffee or the spanking.

And just like that their casual flirty relationship seemed to be back on track. Jameson settled himself at his usual spot, opened his laptop and prepared to play around with his short stories once more. The wannabe writer was thinking of combining several of them into a full-length novel but he wasn't quite sure that he was headed in the right direction. Fortunately, with the money coming in from Matt's rent he was in no rush to find another source of income so could take his time finding his feet.

That being said, he didn't seem to be accomplishing much at present. It didn't help that he was distracted; constantly sneaking furtive glances at the counter to watch Nicolas as he worked.

What am I waiting for?

3

That evening when Jameson returned home, he discovered a message on his answering machine that made his day. In fact, it was the best news he'd had in months. The woman who'd stolen his credit card details had finally been apprehended and had already pleaded guilty, meaning there'd be no trial. Her name was Lila Jacobs and she'd formerly worked at a charming weekend retreat in the mountains that Jameson and David had gone to for their last anniversary, which was now a bittersweet memory in itself. Apparently, she had done the same to around fifty or so other unsuspecting guests of the resort and had spent several hundred thousand dollars before being caught.

It was such a huge relief to Jameson that he did a little dance of joy around the answering machine. Granted, the bank had already reimbursed him for the fraudulent expenses but it was still wonderful to hear of the conviction of the criminal who had created them. Especially, after Jameson had had to go through the onerous task of going through all his statements to identify all the illegal purchases, although it had also revealed that his penchant for shoes was slightly more costly than he'd been aware – well, that he'd allowed himself to believe at any rate.

He immediately rang Ruby to tell her the good news.

"Glad they caught the bitch! Cocktails?" Her response was, as always, perfect.

They agreed to meet at The Cat's Meow – a popular cocktail bar not far from Jameson's townhouse. It was a cozy little hole-in-the-wall, with a wonderfully kitsch vibe. The staff were always super-friendly, particularly the owner, a handsome chap by the name of Az who always wore magnificently tight t-shirts and was quite generous with his alcohol. As usual, it was bustling with a mixed crowd of gays, straights and everything in between, which filled the bar with a friendly babble of conversation.

After about an hour, Jameson and Ruby were becoming rather tipsy from the delightfully strong cocktails. They had just managed to score a corner booth and were settling into their fourth round of drinks when Jameson caught sight of Nicolas walking in the front door. A smile immediately sprang to his face, as it usually did in the presence of the object of his affection.

"What are you grinning about?" asked Ruby teasingly.

Jameson pointed out Nicolas. He'd already prattled on more than a few times about his coffice crush.

"Scrumptious! So why haven't you asked him out yet?" she inquired in her forthright fashion.

"I'm not sure if he likes me. Besides, I'm not ready," said Jameson self-consciously.

"Bullshit! You're just scared because of what those bastards did to you, but you can't be afraid for the rest of your life. You need to put yourself out there," insisted Ruby.

"I know," agreed Jameson begrudgingly.

"Well, what are you waiting for?"

"What? Now?!?"

"Yes!"

"No, I can't."

"Yes, you can. You're a catch; he'd be a fool not to see it. Go and do it now!"

"But if he says no then I will have to find another café."

"Seriously, are in you in high school?"

"It'd be awkward."

"Stop setting yourself up for failure before you even try. Be a grown up and go ask the handsome man out."

Jameson knew well from experience that Ruby wouldn't let up until he gave in.

"OK, OK. I surrender, but if he shoots me down you're buying the drinks for the rest of tonight."

"Done. Now get your cute little butt over there!"

Reluctantly, Jameson got up and made his way over to where Nicolas was standing at the corner of the bar, chatting to an attractive, flaxen-haired gentleman. He was just about tap Nicolas on the shoulder when the beautiful barista leaned forward to kiss his companion. When Jameson saw that is was far more than a friendly peck he felt a sickly, sinking feeling in the pit of his stomach. He quickly hightailed it back to Ruby before Nicolas had a chance to see him.

Ruby, who had seen what had occurred, had a sympathetic look upon her face.

"I'm sorry I pushed you," said Ruby in an apologetic tone.

"Forget it. It's fine," replied Jameson, although his face probably betrayed his disappointment.

Clearly distraught, Jameson downed the rest of his cocktail.

"Well, plenty more roosters in the barn," said Ruby, attempting to keep the mood light.

"I think I'm going to go," said Jameson suddenly.

"Do you want to go to another bar?"

"No, I think I'll just go home. Thanks for the cocktails."

Jameson quickly kissed Ruby goodbye on the cheek and practically fled from the bar, leaving his friend behind with a worried look upon her face.

* * *

Once outside, Jameson rushed down the street, all the while silently berating himself for not approaching Nicolas earlier.

You had plenty of chances and now he's probably already in love and going to get married!

Jameson knew he was being a touch melodramatic but he was too wrapped up in self-pity to care. His next thought was to buy a gallon of ice cream and eat himself into a nice little diabetic coma so he didn't have to deal with his overwrought emotions.

Indeed, he had every intention of doing just that when he spied a quite muscular man across the street, heading into one of the gates to Janeway Park. Jameson recognized him as one of the regulars at Sweat Station. Given the late hour

Jameson assumed that the gent in question was out for something more than a pleasant evening stroll.

Of a daytime, Janeway Park was a wonderful spot for picnics, running and sun baking, but it proved just as popular at night, with the more wooded area to the north of the park crawling with men, strangers, eager to give each other a friendly helping hand. One of the reasons that it was so well-frequented was due to all the like-minded gentlemen that lived just across the road at Graywood Gardens and who often popped out for a late night snack.

Jameson suddenly decided that instead of falling back into his bad habit of comfort eating he'd try the good old-fashioned method of boosting one's deflated self-esteem – hot anonymous sex. He crossed the road, entered the park and started briskly along the path towards the center of the action. Up ahead he could see the muscular form of the man from the gym disappearing into the undergrowth at the side. Jameson decided to walk just a little bit further along, as he preferred to make this encounter as anonymous as possible. He just wanted to forget about his feelings and lose himself in the chase.

It had been years since he'd been cruising and the anticipation of what was to come had already begun to push thoughts of Nicolas and missed opportunities to the side. Jameson stepped away from the footpath and followed one of the tracks to the side that had been made by the feet of many men in their pursuit of passion.

As he walked through the bushes, Jameson heard the occasional rustling of leaves as bodies moved through the trees mixed in with low voices and light moans. His cock began to stir within the confines of his jeans as the excitement of being on the hunt took hold.

Jameson had been wandering for about ten minutes or so and while he had glimpsed quite a few men prowling about there wasn't anyone who really took his fancy. That is, until he saw two muscle bears, with their pants undone, masturbating one another. The pair looked to be in their mid-thirties – although with the low lighting it was hard to be sure – both with beards and cropped hair. They turned when they heard his footsteps, crunching through the fallen leaves, and motioned for him to join them.

The bulge in Jameson's pants continued to grow as he approached the pair and could see their man-sized members jutting out of their open jeans. Without needing to be asked Jameson sunk to his knees and grabbed hold of a cock in each hand. Both the manhoods were thick and around eight inches in length, with the one on the left dribbling a small trail of precum. Jameson's mouth began to water and he wasted no time in diving face-first onto their eager erections, moving his mouth from one to the other…licking, nibbling and sucking. It had been so long since he'd fellated anyone, let alone a random stranger, and he went about his work with gusto, encouraged by their appreciative moans and the feel of their rough hands pressing down on his head and shoulders.

After a few minutes, Jameson felt the strong hands grabbing hold of him, then lifting him, as the duo pulled him to his feet and into a passionate three-way kiss.

"You're beautiful," said the one with the small tribal tattoo on his neck.

"Thanks," replied Jameson, always happy to receive a compliment.

"You want to come back to our place for a proper play?" asked the other man.

Jameson appeared a little hesitant, as it wasn't what he'd planned and he'd never been in the habit going home with men he'd met in such places.

"We only live just across the road " the tattooed man reassured him.

The feel of his throbbing erection straining against his zipper and the memory of their delicious dicks, tempted Jameson to throw caution to the wind and accept their kind offer.

"Yes, I'd love to!" Jameson's libido was now fully in charge.

As they left the undergrowth and walked back through the park the trio made small talk.

"I'm Finn and this is my husband Tom," said the tattooed man.

"Jameson, nice to meet you."

Jameson always tried his best to be polite no matter the situation. In the brighter lighting he could see that his new playmates were not as similar as he'd first thought. While they were both quite muscular and hirsute, with clear blue eyes, Tom had paler skin and jet-black hair to Finn's far lighter brunette locks and honey-brown tan.

A few minutes later, they had crossed the street and entered the main foyer of Graywood Gardens. After a short elevator ride, they arrived at the 11th floor and were inside the couple's apartment seconds later. Once the front door was shut behind them the trio came together kissing and pulling at each other's clothing, stripping one another as Tom and Finn slowly led Jameson to their bedroom. In an instant, the threesome was fully naked and rolling together in a mess of writhing limbs on the king-sized bed.

For his part, Jameson was completely lost in the moment. After his self-imposed celibacy it was heavenly to have not one but two strapping specimens to play with. The muscle bears sandwiched Jameson between their firm bodies and ravaged his body…kissing, biting and tasting his fine form. Their hairy chests rubbed against the smooth skin of Jameson's torso.

The duo slowly worked their way down their captive's defined body, making Jameson squirm as their mouths pleasured him. When they reached crotch level Tom easily engulfed Jameson's solid erection with his warm mouth, while Finn spread Jameson's plump, yet firm, ass cheeks and shoved his face deep inside.

Jameson cried out in ecstasy as the two mouths went about their dual attack. He felt his left leg being raised to allow Finn even wider access to his sensitive rosebud – it had been so long since he'd been touched there it was practically virginal again. All this stimulation after so much abstinence was more than Jameson could bear and after only a few minutes of such wonderful treatment his body tensed in orgasm. Jameson gripped the back of Tom's head as he shot his load into the eager mouth, which greedily swallowed down every last drop.

Both of the couple slid back up and gave Jameson another long passionate three-way kiss.

"Delicious," growled Tom.

"Sorry, I came so quickly," apologized Jameson, slightly embarrassed by his rapid release.

"That's fine. Besides we aren't done with you yet," replied Finn, with a wicked wink and a smile.

Jameson was about to protest and make his excuses to leave but then the duo moved back down and recommenced their work. Any ideas of leaving soon faded away as Tom slowly coaxed Jameson's spent manhood back to life, nibbling on his foreskin and swirling his head around the hypersensitive cock head, while Finn continued on with his exploration of his new toy's ever-so-tight ass.

They rolled their guest onto his back and Finn kept Jameson's muscular legs spread wide and in the air. Tom maneuvered around into a sixty-nine position so that he could continue to worship Jameson's growing member while receiving a similar service.

Jameson eagerly took to the task at hand and was soon corkscrewing up and down the thick shaft while using his left hand to fondle Tom's hairy balls. The untamed black pubic hair tickled his nose and chin as he ground his face deep into Tom's crotch. He loved the masculine scent that flooded his nostrils. Jameson moved his hands around to the furry globes of Tom's buttocks and squeezed them as he pulled Tom in closer. Nicolas was the furthest thing from Jameson's mind as he pleasured and was pleasured in return. All those months of having nothing but his hand for relief had made him insatiable and desperate to sate his carnal longings.

Tom moved slightly downward and Jameson could feel the two mouths fighting for access to his hole. Their tongues battled together, both trying to open him up. Their beards felt divine as they rubbed across the sensitive area, causing Jameson to moan even louder.

Suddenly, Finn stood up and went to the bedside drawers. Jameson guessed that he was getting himself some protection and was proved correct when he felt thick fingers coating the entrance of his ass with lubricant before he felt a latex-covered cock head pushed up against his exposed hole.

Jameson didn't mind that Finn hadn't bothered to ask if he wanted to be fucked. To tell the truth after all that rimming he was aching to be penetrated and pounded hard. He grunted as the cock head forced its way inside, followed slowly by inch after glorious inch. The tightness of his passage gradually eased as it adjusted to the invader. Jameson felt thoroughly stuffed at both ends and loved every second of it.

Finn started to pump Jameson's ass, slowly at first, then building up to a steady pace. The room echoed with sounds of slapping skin and the guttural grunts of men at play. They stayed locked in this passionate tableau for a good fifteen minutes.

"My turn?" asked Tom, clearly eager for a ride of Jameson's delicious derrière.

His husband appeared keen to oblige, so they swapped positions, flipping Jameson onto his hands and knees with Tom taking him from behind while Finn plowed into Jameson's open mouth. Jameson adored being spit-roasted. They slammed in to him again and again, his muffled moans getting louder as the intensity of the rhythm increased.

Jameson felt the sweat dripping down off of the pair as they leaned forward to kiss each other over Jameson's back. He felt a momentary pang on jealousy over their relationship but brushed it aside and gave into the delicious carnality.

Suddenly Finn removed his member from Jameson's hungry mouth and went to the open bedside drawer to get more supplies. Jameson wasn't sure what was planned until Finn reached down and rolled a condom onto Jameson's engorged cock. He then slid down onto the bed underneath Jameson and offered up his ass. Tom stopped fucking long enough for Jameson to line up and sink his solid eight uncut inches deep inside the waiting hole. The trio quickly became even sweatier as their bodies repeatedly collided together. The grunts and gasps of the three men filled the room as they indulged their animal instincts…clawing, biting and feeding off one another.

Tom's masterful fucking of his ass and the way Finn was milking Jameson's cock with his velvety passage soon had Jameson at the brink of climax once more. He pumped harder and was rewarded by a burst of pleasure as his cock exploded into its protective sheath.

Tom pulled out and discarded his condom and Jameson soon followed suit. Finn pulled Jameson down to the bed and Tom lay down on the other side to sandwich their guest again. The muscle bears began to wank furiously and soon sprayed their hot loads onto Jameson's slick skin. When the last spurts of cream subsided, they moved in even closer together, kissing and running their hands lazily over one another's tired bodies.

The threesome lay like this for some minutes as the sweat, saliva and semen dried together in a sticky mess between them.

Jameson hadn't been held like that in so long and it felt so good…he never wanted to leave.

"Do you want to stay the night?" asked Tom, as if reading Jameson's thoughts.

Jameson hesitated an instant before answering, not sure if that was the best idea, as the intimacy may bring up memories of David.

What if I start crying?

Once again, Jameson decided the risk was worth the companionship. It felt good to have meaningless uncomplicated fun with no risk of heartbreak.

"Yes, please," replied Jameson, feeling safe and secure.

"Great," whispered Tom, before giving Jameson a peck on his lips.

"You were definitely a find," added Finn.

None of them showed the slightest interest in getting up to shower, so the trio soon drifted off into a contented sleep, with their bodies comfortably entangled and their urges sated.

The following morning Jameson woke up to the pleasing sensation of a blow job. He sleepily looked down and saw Finn hard at work. Behind him, Jameson could feel Tom's erection pressing into his buttocks. Before too long the boys resumed their activities of the night before and some ten minutes later, three fresh loads coated the boys' skin.

Following a lazy, and thoroughly enjoyable, group shower, the three men were sitting at the dining table, chatting and enjoying a delicious breakfast...Jameson having eagerly agreed to their gracious offer of something to eat before he went off on his merry way.

Their conversation was pleasant and Jameson found that he rather liked the pair of them...and not just for their skilled manipulations of his body. He discovered that they'd been married for three years and together for fifteen. Their clearly loving relationship made him a tad morose. His feelings of jealousy came trickling back and he did his best to not think of the life he'd lost with David ...or the thought of Nicolas waking up next to the Adonis from the bar.

Jameson knew he was far too young to be so bitter and cynical but it was a hard mindset to break. Eventually, he roused himself to action and left the boys so he could get back into his daily routine. Jameson did, however, promise to keep in touch – as friends if nothing else. He didn't think it would be wise to become a regular playmate, as his feelings were already a bit confused and Jameson was cautious of intruding in their relationship.

He headed downstairs and as he exited the building he passed by Perk Up, which understandably turned his thoughts back to Nicolas. Jameson didn't know what he wanted but thought he should maybe stay away from the café for a few days until he'd had a chance to think.

I don't want to act like a total idiot the next time I see him.

* * *

Over the next few days, Jameson decided to keep himself busy to stop him from constantly dwelling on the beautiful barista. To this end, he went up into the overly stuffed attic and started to sort through the mountains of boxes and junk that had been accumulated with each generation. He'd been putting it off for years, as he knew that it would take some time, but it proved to be the perfect diversion.

Jameson's hard work was rewarded with several interesting discoveries, including a beautiful large mahogany desk, which contained a batch of small, red leather-bound journals written by his great-grandfather, who was quite the wordsmith. In fact, Jameson became so wrapped up in reading through them that he lost track of the time and had to race to the gym to make the stretch class with his favorite instructor – Avery. The handsome teacher was not only a delight to look at, with his tall, lean defined build, flowing blond locks and wise gray eyes, but was rather adept at encouraging those in his class to stretch further than they'd thought humanly possible.

Jameson was rather happy with his progress at the gym – an opinion shared by quite a few people given the admiring glances he'd been getting of late. Indeed, he was looking the fittest he'd ever been but his muscles ached from all his dedicated work on the weights floor, and needed more than just the quick stretches he'd been doing between sets. Hence he'd started going to Avery's class, about a month beforehand, and he was delighted to find his flexibility ever increasing…you never knew when being able to put your feet past your ears would come in handy, after all.

Arriving just as the class was starting, Jameson saw that Connor had set up a mat for him in the front row – a coveted position as one was able to pay close attention to Avery's stunning physique as he lead them through their exercises. Jameson had met Connor a few weeks previously when Avery had put the class into pairs for some partner-assisted stretches. Connor was a handsome lad; although his floppy brown hair and kind, brown eyes framed by thick red frames gave him a slight air of geekiness – somewhat appropriate given his work as a web designer. His friendly, easygoing manner quickly endeared him to Jameson and the pair started to train together on the gym floor – neither of them having a regular training partner – as well as catching up outside of class.

At twenty-three, Connor was only a few years younger than Jameson and it wasn't long before they found themselves confiding in each other like old friends, bonding over failed past relationships and a mutual love of Doctor Who. There was something so trusting and honest about Connor that made Jameson open up to him. Jameson had been sorely lacking a male confidante since Judd's betrayal and Connor seemed to be the perfect replacement for his traitorous ex-best friend. Not to say that he didn't dearly value his close friendship with Ruby but there were just some things it was easier to discuss with another like-minded guy. That aside, Jameson had a suspicion that Ruby and Connor would get along fabulously, something, which was proved right, after Jameson had introduced them over a scrumptious Sunday brunch.

There wasn't anything romantic about their relationship; however, as Connor was wildly in love with his tailor boyfriend, Didier. Jameson had, of course, had some less than pure thoughts about his new friend, especially after the first time they'd gone into the steam room together after class. After they sat down, Jameson had casually glanced down at Connor's naked lap – an ingrained instinct of comparison that all men engage in – and seen a sleeping monster. Not that Jameson was a size queen but he certainly appreciated when the gods blessed boys with ample appendages. Jameson's own cock had stirred at the sight but he positioned his towel to cover it as best he could, although judging by the appreciative looks that Jameson noticed amongst the other steamers, he wasn't the only one impressed by the sizable manhood.

The class was challenging, as usual, and by the end both Jameson and Connor were tired and sweaty but feeling much more supple. After they indulged in their customary post-class steaming, the two friends headed downstairs to the café next-door – Dom's Delights – to have protein smoothies and split a triple chocolate muffin…everyone knows that the calories barely count if you're sharing. As usual the place was packed with gym members either rewarding themselves for a job well done or indulging in treats they were about to go burn off. The brightly lit café buzzed with the sound of happy customers gossiping and munching away, as the wonderfully comforting smell of fresh baked, butterscotch goodness wafted through the air. By the time their order arrived they were well into Jameson's retelling of his disappointment over Nicolas and the consequent satisfying sexcapades.

"Man, that's sounds hot!" exclaimed Connor, clearly a little jealous of his friend's recent conquest.

"Well it was unexpected, but good," replied Jameson, a little smugly.

"Are you going to see them again?" asked Connor, before shoving a deliciously moist piece of chocolate muffin into his hungry mouth.

"I don't know, maybe. It was the most fun I've had in a long time but…"

"Nicolas?"

Connor had already heard numerous times about Jameson's infatuation with the barista.

"Yeah. I can't stop thinking about him but I think I've left it too late."

"You don't know that for sure. Maybe it was just a casual kiss. When are you going to see him again?"

"At the end of the week I think."

"Well then you can just ask him about the kiss then."

"I don't know. I don't want to come across as all stalkery," said Jameson, in a half-joking manner, as he grabbed the last bite of the muffin and swallowed down its chocolaty perfection.

"What's the worst that can happen? You'll find out if he's still available or not and it will put you out of your misery one way or another," reasoned Connor.

"I guess I'm scared of getting hurt again," said Jameson, sounding every bit as vulnerable as he felt.

"Understandable. But you can't expect to find love again if you aren't willing to take a chance. Besides, you're hot. If I was single I'd be on you like a shot!"

"Thanks, right back at you."

The talk then turned to lighter matters, such as the scandalously, skimpy shorts that Avery had been wearing.

"Honestly, he should just do the class naked," said Connor.

"No arguments here," agreed Jameson.

Their easy camaraderie always improved Jameson's mood. Jameson knew that Connor was right and he felt encouraged by his friend's faith in him. He vowed to himself that the next time he saw Nicolas he'd man up and ask the beautiful barista out on a date.

* * *

Some days later, Jameson worked up the nerve to go back to Perk Up and see if he still had a chance with the bubbly barista.

"Hey JJ, where you been?" said Nic, greeting Jameson with a welcoming white smile.

"JJ?" asked Jameson, a little taken aback by the new nickname.

"Thought I'd try something new. You don't like it?" replied the barista, his brow furrowed in concern.

"No…I mean…yes, I do." Daniel was a little flustered. "It's just that nobody has ever called me that before."

"So I'm the first, I'm honored."

Nicolas gave him a saucy wink. Jameson blushed a little and felt himself relax. It appeared all his fretting had been for naught and his flirty relationship with Nicolas seemed as full of innuendo as ever. They continued on in their small talk, all the while Jameson was dying to ask what had happened between Nicolas and the handsome stranger the other night. He forced himself to wait a few minutes before he brought up the subject.

"Did you have fun at The Cat's Meow on Friday?" he asked in as casual manner as he could muster.

"You were there? Why didn't you come and say hi?" asked Nicolas, seeming slightly offended and possibly a little disappointed.

"Well you were kind of attached at the mouth to someone," said Jameson, in what he hoped was a teasing tone.

"Oh Sean! He was a lot of fun. We'd been chatting online for a few weeks and that was the first time we met up."

"Looks like it was a success then."

Jameson was desperate to know what had happened but at the same time dreading the answer.

"Yeah, we've actually seen each other every day this week. Kinda unexpected but really good as well," said Nicolas, apparently oblivious to the heartbreak he was inflicting.

"That's great." Jameson determinedly plastered a big smile on his face, which he hoped disguised the crushing disappointment he felt inside.

Jameson carried his order to his habitual spot and switched on his laptop. He sat there looking at the screen wanting to lose himself in the story he'd been working on, but he was so distraught that he only ended up reading the same paragraph over and over again. His mind whirled with thoughts but they had nothing to do with his writing.

Why did I wait so long? Maybe it's for the best. Do you really need your heart stomped on again? I need to stop being such a soppy schoolboy!

After an hour of wasted time he came to a decision and pulled out his phone. A few text messages later he packed up his belongings and bid adieu to Nicolas. Instead of heading home Jameson turned into the apartment building and was soon buzzed up to the 11th floor where Tom and Finn were no doubt eagerly waiting to take all his troubles away once more.

* * *

A few wonderfully exhausting hours later Jameson headed home, after politely declining his new friends' offer to spend the night with them. Strangely, the encounter, while pleasurable, hadn't quite managed to fully take his mind off of Nicolas.

Why am I so hung up on him?

It was a question Jameson kept coming back to. He didn't know why he felt such a pull towards the barista – apart from his beautiful face/body/personality – well, maybe he did have an inkling. Fortunately, Perk Up was closed by the time he'd finished with the boys so he didn't run the risk of encountering his crush again that evening…as much as he wanted to.

As Jameson walked home he didn't know quite what to with himself. He didn't feel like being alone in the townhouse – he knew that both Trent and Matt were working late that night – with his emotions in such a turbulent state, but he had no place else to go. He thought of calling Connor and relaying his tale of woe but he didn't feel up to going through it all again tonight. In any event, he was saved from further worry by a timely phone call from Ruby, who had an intriguing offer for him.

"How would you like to give a slimy banker a taste of justice?" teased Ruby.

"Sounds perfect!" answered Jameson, grateful to have a new distraction.

"Can I come over tonight and tell you about the case?"

"Sure I'll be home in about fifteen minutes."

"Great, I'll see you then."

Excited by the prospect of a spot of vengeance Jameson raced home and prepared some snacks – rice crackers and an array of dips – and opened a bottle of wine that he'd had chilling in the fridge.

Since the first time with Marcus, Jameson had helped Ruby out with another three cases of unfaithful spouses – apparently infidelity was in the air – each time a rousing success. Granted, the idea of revenge thrilled him more than he cared to admit but he figured that as long as bad guys were being punished there was nothing wrong with it. Besides his foray into righting wrongs was undoubtedly helping lighten the load of the emotional baggage he'd been lugging around for the past several months. If he couldn't punish David and Judd at least he was exacting revenge on others of their kind.

Ruby arrived, looking exactly like a femme fatale from a film noir, with her hair and makeup styled to perfection. Her deep blue dress clung to her curves in a way that fairly demanded the attention of anyone in the vicinity. Even Jameson, whose leanings were firmly towards the male of the species, wasn't completely immune to her charms.

"Rosé?" offered Jameson, handing his guest a rather full glass.

"Why thank you, kind sir," Ruby purred in her most seductive honey-laden voice. Once settled on the sofa with their drinks the twosome settled into easy conversation.

"So, who are we taking down this time?" said Jameson with a childlike glee.

"A particularly despicable gent by the name of Bartholomew Kingsley III."

"Well with a name like that what else could he be?" joked Jameson.

"Basically he had an affair with one of his junior analysts, stole several of her ideas, then fired her and threatened to blackball her in the industry if she made a fuss."

"Sounds like a real gem," remarked Jameson sarcastically.

"Apparently, what he did to her is just a small sampling of his dastardly behavior. Our client, Veronica Masters, is the lovely lass in question. Ideally, she'd like her job back and see Mr Kingsley punished in some manner. Unfortunately, she doesn't have any proof, which is where we come in."

"How can I help?"

"It turns out that Kingsley plays for both sides of the field, and has some rather perverse proclivities, something his very conservative family and employers wouldn't be too pleased to hear."

Jameson had a sudden pricking of his conscience.

"I'm not sure I'm comfortable outing someone, no matter what they've done," said Jameson, his unease apparent.

"Don't worry, we wouldn't go that far but some compromising photos should be enough leverage to get our client what she wants," reassured Ruby, in a matter-of-fact manner.

"OK. I guess that works."

Jameson wasn't completely convinced but he was still curious to see what Ruby had in mind. They spent the next hour hashing out the plan and making their way through two bottles of wine. By the time Jameson showed Ruby out he was feeling a bit fuzzy, but much more content than he'd been earlier in the evening. He drank a large bottle of water before heading up to his bedroom, as he wanted to avoid the annoyance of being hung-over the next day.

As he lay in his comfortable large bed Jameson ran over his part in the upcoming plan. He still had some niggling worries as to the questionable morality of what they were going to do but felt that Kingsley probably had earned this particular karmic retribution. Sleep came quickly but despite the distraction of the new project one last thought flickered across his mind before he reached the land of slumber.

Nicolas.

* * *

As he prowled the red-lit corridors Jameson could feel hungry eyes upon him. Understandably so, given that his carefully chosen all-black outfit, consisting of a leather harness, heavy army-style boots and skintight PVC pants showed off his gym-honed body to perfection. Through the thin walls he could hear the agreeable sounds of male pleasure, accompanied by the familiar scent of sex in the air. His manhood stirred in his pants, anxious to take part in the manly games.

Despite the substantial undisguised interest of others, Jameson had eyes for only one man – Bartholomew Kingsley III. It took him ten minutes to find his target loitering around the glory hole section, obviously searching for fun. Even if Jameson hadn't been looking for Bartholomew, he would certainly be hard to miss with his tall imposing build, tousled blond hair, bright green eyes and youthful features that belied his approaching middle age. Jameson couldn't help but admire Bartholomew's muscular frame, which was clad only in a red and black jockstrap, matching knee-high socks and black sneakers.

OK, it's now or never!

Taking a deep breath Jameson mentally prepared himself and walked right up to Bartholomew, roughly pushed him up against the wall and slapped him across the face.

"Ready to play, boy?" Jameson asked in a gruff voice.

"Yes, Sir!" barked Bartholomew in response, the excitement apparent in his voice.

"Good. Come!"

Jameson grabbed the muscular man by the arm and forcefully pulled him along the corridor and down the stairs to a small playroom on the basement level. Once there, Jameson shoved Bartholomew inside and locked the door behind them, ready to finish the job he'd been sent there to do.

Ironically, it was Bartholomew himself who had provided them with the perfect opportunity to find justice for their client. During his brief affair with Veronica he'd let slip a few incriminating details during their post-coital chats. Veronica, in turn, had given Ruby a wealth of information that had enabled them to formulate their plan. It turned out the brash banker frequented a popular sex club – ManHole – for their regular Thursday fetish evening, where he liked to indulge his submissive side. Apparently, he loved to be dominated just as much as he enjoyed lording it over others during his regular life.

Fortunately, Jameson was no stranger to the kinkier side of life and was more than willing to play the part in order to extract the leverage they needed. He had quite enjoyed his earlier forays into role-playing, which had come to a stop after he'd met David, who, regrettably, hadn't been a fan of such games.

"Strip!" commanded Jameson.

Bartholomew hastily removed his jockstrap, socks and shoes, and stood before Jameson, naked and obviously eager to comply. His rock-hard erection showing just how much he was enjoying being under Jameson's control.

Jameson grabbed hold of Bartholomew by the arm and half-dragged him to wooden stocks set up in the right corner. Jameson had done a spot of reconnaissance work a few days beforehand to find the right spot for his task.

"Take your place, boy!" Jameson growled.

Bartholomew silently obeyed, bent forward and placed his head and wrists in the proper position. Jameson efficiently locked his willing captive in place – he'd had a little practice with a like-minded friend some years before. Despite the fact that he was focused on the task at hand, Jameson's cock strained against the tight confines of his PVC pants. Bartholomew's chiseled muscular frame and subservient position were arousing to say the least. Jameson would have loved to give in to his base carnal urges and violate the inviting muscular bubble butt but that wasn't what he was there to do.

Instead, he raised his hand and swung it down, loudly smacking the bare buttocks before him. Bartholomew grunted in appreciation. Jameson repeated his action, again and again, and was soon rewarded with the appearance of bright red hand prints on the pale skin.

"You like that whore?" Jameson taunted his captive between hits.

"Yes, Sir!"

Bartholomew was evidently enjoying himself immensely.

"Do you deserve it, boy?"

"Yes, Sir!"

"Why, boy?"

"Because I'm a dirty slut, Sir."

Sweat began to slowly drip down Jameson's chest from the effort. After a few minutes Jameson's hand began to ache, so he decided to change tactics. He grabbed hold of Bartholomew's dangling balls and pulled down hard.

"Ahhhh fuck!" cried Bartholomew, in an apparent mixture of pleasure and pain. "Thank you, Sir!"

Bartholomew squirmed, gasped and moaned as Jameson continued to work on him. Jameson teased and tortured his helpless prisoner over the next hour, tweaking his big brown nipples, slapping his painfully red ass, biting and scratching all over his magnificent body, all the while calling Bartholomew all sorts of names.

Truthfully, Jameson became a little lost in the game. The dominant persona had well and truly taken hold. In his mind it wasn't just Bartholomew he was punishing but David, Judd and all others of their ilk. Jameson felt powerful and firmly in control – something he'd been desperately missing – and he relished every second of it. Inflicting pain on this traitorous bastard was definitely cathartic.

Both their bodies were slick were perspiration and the air in the room was heavy with a manly musk. Bartholomew had red marks all over his pale skin and his legs were visibly shaking from being kept in the same position for such an extended time, although the precum dripping from his beer-can thick inches was ample evidence of his enjoyment.

Jameson decided it was time to finish his job. He reached into his left boot, retrieved the mini-camera that Ruby had given him, placed it on the small padded bench at the side just out of Bartholomew's line of vision and switched it on. Jameson moved in front of the stocks and grabbed Bartholomew's face by the chin.

"It's time to confess your sins, boy!" Jameson thundered.

"I don't know what you mean, Sir," replied Bartholomew, slightly confused.

Jameson spit in his face.

"Yes, you do, boy! Why do you need to be punished?"

Jameson's voice now contained an unmistakable malice.

"Because I'm bad, Sir!" replied Bartholomew, still playing the game.

"I know that boy! I want to know how bad you've been. You want to please me don't you boy?"

"Yes Sir," came Bartholomew's meek reply.

"Then tell me what you've done."

"I...I...I don't recycle."

"That's pathetic! Not good enough boy!" shouted Jameson, as he took Bartholomew's balls in his firm grip once more and yanked them downward much harder than before.

"Fucking hell!" screamed his captive.

"Now tell me something decent or I will find the fattest, hairiest grandpa to come in here and fuck that worthless ass of yours!" threatened Jameson.

"No, Sir. Please, Sir," begged Bartholomew with a pleading look in his eyes.

"Then answer my question."

"I've cheated people!"

"That's better. Go on, boy."

Soon Bartholomew was spilling secrets left, right and center in an obvious attempt to please his newfound Master. Ten minutes later Jameson had more than enough ammunition.

"That's enough, boy. You've done well."

His voice had taken on a much more soothing tone.

"Thank you, Sir," said Bartholomew humbly.

"Veronica will be pleased," continued Jameson, his voice practically dripping with venom.

"What?" Bartholomew's face registered a slight alarm.

"You remember her, don't you?" asked Jameson in a mocking manner.

"What the hell is going on?" demanded Bartholomew, the previous subservient tone completely gone from his voice.

"Just a little payback."

Jameson then brandished the camera in front of his captive.

"Let me out now!" yelled Bartholomew.

In response, Jameson slapped Bartholomew hard across the face once more.

"Calm down Mr Kingsley. I'm just here to work out a little deal."

"I'm going to get you for this. I'll kill you, faggot!" Bartholomew's manner became loud and menacing.

Moving quickly, Jameson retrieved Bartholomew's jockstrap from the floor and shoved it into his captive's mouth to stop him from attracting undue attention. Now that Bartholomew's threats of violence were successfully muffled Jameson was able to continue.

"Such language! I'm going to stand here until you're ready to hear what I have to say," said Jameson grinning smugly.

Bartholomew's face was flushed red with anger as he tried in vain to yell for help. A few minutes passed before he apparently realized the futility of his actions and he stopped making noise.

"Ready to listen?" asked Jameson, with the gentle condescending tone one normally reserves for naughty children.

Bartholomew nodded his head in agreement, although his eyes were still full of murderous rage.

"Here's what is going to happen. You are going to stop badmouthing Veronica to your colleagues and write her a sterling letter of recommendation. Otherwise, this video is going to find its way to your board of directors. Understand?"

A thoroughly defeated looking Bartholomew nodded his head.

"The same punishment applies if you try to seek retribution on Veronica or myself. Are we clear?" asked Jameson, as he removed the jockstrap from Bartholomew's mouth.

"Yes!" he spat.

"Good. Well I think we're done here."

Jameson, put the camera back into his boot and prepared to leave.

"Aren't you going to let me out?" asked Bartholomew in a panicked voice, as he struggled against the stocks. He had the desperate aura of a trapped animal

"I don't think that'd be wise. Don't worry I'll send someone to set you free…in a little while."

Jameson placed the jockstrap back in Bartholomew's mouth to stop the torrent of abuse that had begun anew. He exited the room, shut the door behind him and continued along the corridor. At the top of the stairs he almost ran into a handsome blond muscle bear. In a fit of benevolence

Jameson decided to bestow a little kindness upon Bartholomew.

"If you go to the playroom with the stocks there's a guy who could really use your help," Jameson suggested.

"Thanks!"

The muscle bear smiled and gave Jameson's pert buttocks a light squeeze before he headed downstairs.

Jameson made his way to the cloakroom to retrieve his bag and t-shirt and quickly exited the club. He thought it best if he was long-gone by the time Bartholomew was released.

On the way back to his car Jameson rang Ruby and told her of his success. He was feeling rather pleased with himself and was still riding the high of the power trip. They arranged to meet the following day so he could hand over the camera and celebrate their success.

ManHole was only a short drive from his townhouse and fifteen minutes later he was walking through his front door, grateful to be home. He bounded up the stairs, stripped out of his clothes and proceeded to have a nice long hot shower. As he soaped himself up his thoughts turned back to Bartholomew. As despicable as Jameson found him, he couldn't deny that his former prisoner was certainly hot. It didn't take much before Jameson was at full mast, pleasuring himself to the thoughts of what else he could have done to his cocky captive. A few minutes later, Jameson braced himself against the wet tiles of the shower wall as his body shook with orgasm. His semen violently spurted up and then back down, following the water swirling down the drain.

Jameson finished up and toweled himself off before heading to alluring embrace of his bed. As he slid between the white Egyptian cotton sheets and moved his head to find the comfy spot on his pillows he began to reflect on his actions. While he had certainly enjoyed righting wrongs, he felt a little empty as the glow of the vengeance faded. He began to reconsider if what he was doing was really helping him or, indeed, if he was suited to it at all. The thrill of it just wasn't exciting him as much anymore. Jameson had no doubt that Marcus, Bartholomew and the others had gotten their comeuppance but it wasn't making him deal with his own issues.

In his heart Jameson knew what he wanted more than revenge was another chance at love, although the object of his affection remained seemingly out of reach.

Why can't he be mine?

4

Sunlight flooded into the attic through the big circle window. Specks of dust danced and swirled in the light as Jameson sat at the big mahogany desk, typing away on his laptop. The view through the window itself gave out towards the nearby mountain range and overlooked his garden – a particularly inspiring sight today given that Matt and Trent were sun baking au naturel. Jameson didn't mind them doing such, as he often did it himself of a summertime when he didn't feel like traipsing all the way out to Murdoch Beach. He could hear the gentle murmur of their conversation and thought to join them in an hour or so when he had finished a few more pages.

Jameson was indebted to the boys, as they'd been a great help with rearranging the attic and lugging all the rubbish away. Their friendship had continued to grow over the last few months and he enjoyed their company immensely. Indeed, when Matt had timidly asked if Trent could be added to his lease – after he'd only been there for a month – Jameson had raised no objection. Given the amount of time Trent already spent at the townhouse it was hardly a big change. In fact, Jameson was surprised it had taken them so long to ask.

Due to the heat of the day, Jameson was only wearing his small red running shorts, which left very little to the imagination. Even in such skimpy attire the occasional bead of sweat still trickled down his lean, tanned form while he concentrated on the screen before him. Though clearing out the attic had started as a project to keep his mind off of Nicolas – not that it had been particularly effective in that regard – it had provided him with not only a marvelous light and airy space to pursue his career as a writer but also with the much needed direction with which to take his writing. Jameson knew that the work he'd been doing for Ruby wasn't what he really wanted to do forever, even if the last encounter had been quite satisfying, not to mention successful – Bartholomew had been true to his word and Veronica was now gainfully employed in a far better post than the one she'd been forced to leave.

The red, pocket-sized journals he'd found in the desk a few months beforehand were a fascinating read and made him recall tales that his grandfather had told him when he was little. Jameson knew that his great-grandfather, Sébastien James, had been a renowned detective and that they shared the same genetic anomaly that gave them their strikingly mismatched eyes. The journals, however, had given Jameson more of a sense of the man himself and the more he read the more he discovered that he shared quite a few traits with his ascendant. Not only did they share a penchant for writing but also a love of handsome men. In his journals, Sébastien often wrote fondly of his faithful companion, Flynn Reynolds. Indeed, some of the passages were extremely passionate, if not downright pornographic. Jameson had the idea of turning the journals into a series of novels based on their cases – just like Holmes and Watson with the sex scenes included. He knew it was an ambitious undertaking but he felt that he was up to the challenge. Jameson had talked to his parents first, as he didn't want to stir up a family drama if he could help it. They had no problem at all and if anything seemed happy that their son seemed to be getting back on with his life.

Determined to do their stories justice, Jameson decided to do further research and see what he could dig up on the pair. He scoured the Internet and found quite a few digitized newspaper articles detailing their exploits. Jameson also thought it would be interesting to track down any relatives of Flynn to see if they had any more information that he could use. After surfing through a few genealogy websites he discovered that there were several branches of the Reynolds family tree living in the States. Jameson had eagerly sent out a few emails explaining his mission and was delighted when he received a number of replies, including one from a young man living right there in Port Davinica.

His name was Ben Marinos-Reynolds and Flynn had been his grandfather's older brother. Once Jameson told him more about the project he was more than happy to help. It turned out that Ben had been doing his own bit of historical family research, spurred on by the imminent arrival of his first child. The two had soon made a date to meet up at the townhouse so Ben could have a look at the journals and bring over some old family photographs for Jameson to see.

"Hi. You must be Ben, it's nice to…don't I know you?" asked Jameson when he'd first opened the door.

"You do look familiar, but I'm not sure where from," answered Ben, staring a little quizzically at Jameson.

"Anyway, I'm sure it will come to me. Please come in."

The two hit it off straight away. Jameson was attracted to Ben's welcoming open manner and the fact that he was quite handsome with curly brown hair and a muscular build didn't hurt either. Jameson wasn't surprised that Ben had already been snapped up and was evidently happily married.

Why are all the good ones taken?

"They certainly made a dashing duo," exclaimed Jameson, as he flicked through the photos.

"Yep, they were," agreed Ben. "I kinda remember meeting them when I was very little. I'm pretty sure I still have the painted, wooden train set they gave me."

"Your family doesn't mind what I'm planning?" asked Jameson.

"Not at all. They're actually excited. I think they have delusions of becoming famous when it becomes a bestseller," joked Ben.

"I wish!"

Even though he said it jokingly, Jameson wouldn't have said no to a bit of fame and fortune himself.

"You should come by my café sometime and meet my husband, Dom, he's keen to know more about the book as well," suggested Ben.

"Sure…Hold on. Café?" said Jameson, as it suddenly clicked where he'd seen Ben before. "It's not Dom's Delights is it?"

"Yeah….That's it! I remember now, you come in with that cute geeky looking guy. Is that your boyfriend?"

"Connor? No…no, I'm footloose and fancy free."

Jameson tried to cover the tinge of sadness he felt with a slightly forced joviality, as his thoughts became Nicolas-bound once more.

"Well, say hi next time you guys come in and you can have your pick of the pastries!" offered Ben generously.

"Sounds great."

The prospect of complimentary cake helped to mollify Jameson's sudden sad mood. The two then passed an agreeable few hours chatting about their amorous ancestors. That had been three weeks ago and he, and consequently Connor, had since enjoyed the benefits of being friends with the owners of their post-gym stop. Indeed, there always seemed to be a fair few extra biscuits or muffin that miraculously arrived at their table, not that they were complaining mind you.

Jameson pressed save and then shut down his computer, happy with the progress he'd made. If he kept this up he'd be finished by the end of the following month. He made his way downstairs, stopping to grab a towel from the hall cupboard and some ice-cold Cokes from the fridge before joining the boys in the inviting afternoon sun.

* * *

Against his better judgment – and despite having a workspace at home – Jameson still took his laptop to Perk

Up about three times a week, although he didn't tend to stay as long as he had in the past. Try as he might Jameson couldn't get the beautiful barista out of his head. It didn't help that he was confronted with the image of Nicolas gazing sexily down at him from the CocKed posters every time he went to the gym.

Jameson continued to find Nicolas intelligent, witty and altogether captivating, and enjoyed their chats immensely. Nicolas always seemed so genuinely interested in what Jameson was up to. It was all Jameson could do to fight the overwhelming urge to take the charming coffee maker into his arms and confess his undying love.

Even though he knew full well that Nicolas was still seeing Sean, Jameson just couldn't keep away. Mills & Boon fantasies aside, the young writer realized that it wasn't healthy to dwell on someone he couldn't have but it was as if he was powerless to resist. Nicolas' smile never failed brightened his day and every time he heard the barista say "JJ" his heart melted a little more. That being said, every time Nicolas mentioned his boyfriend's name Jameson suffered pangs of intense jealousy.

This tortured state of being was probably the reason why he tossed common sense aside and was considering something quite dangerous – a blind date organized by Ruby.

"You need to put yourself out there," counseled the stylish redhead.

"I know but it's not easy," lamented Jameson.

"At the very least you get a free dinner; the guy's loaded," joked Ruby.

"OK, OK."

Jameson knew that he really had no choice but to give in to her demands.

"Good boy. Now, it's time for another bottle of wine!"

When Dr Rick Manning walked into the restaurant twenty minutes late Jameson was feeling less than impressed. This was compounded, when his date sat straight down without even vaguely attempting to apologize for his tardiness.

Granted, the good doctor was a vision to behold, in a snug navy blue shirt and tailored black pants which showed off his gym-honed physique. His short, light blond hair was immaculately styled and his face was model-perfect, with flawless bright-white teeth, he could have almost passed for a wax doll. Despite his irritation at his date's rudeness, Jameson's cock involuntarily stirred, but these lustful feelings soon went away when they started talking – or rather Rick talked.

"Just a sec," said Rick, responding to his fifth text of the date. When the doctor wasn't talking about himself, he was busy responding to messages from people he obviously considered more important than Jameson. Admittedly, Rick did ask the occasional question of Jameson but somehow always managed to bring it back around to himself.

"…that reminds me of a particularly tricky operation I performed," droned the dreary, self-aggrandizing doctor.

On the plus side, the restaurant – The Spicy Samurai – a relatively new addition to the Port Davinica dining scene, featured a surprisingly tasty Mexican/Japanese fusion menu…the wasabi chicken quesadillas were delectable. Thankfully, their cocktails were as refreshing as they were strong, which Jameson certainly needed to get through the rest of the evening.

It was by far the worst date Jameson had ever been on and that included the time in high school where his date – a surprisingly clumsy footballer – had spilled scalding hot soup onto Jameson's lap, which forced him to spend the rest of the night in the ER with an ice pack on his crotch. Needless to say, their fledgling relationship had ended shortly afterwards.

Jameson waited as long as he could before trying to terminate their evening by signaling the waiter

"Check please."

"It's my treat," said Rick magnanimously.

"Thank you," replied Jameson, thinking that it was the least he deserved after putting up with such appalling behavior.

They collected their jackets from the drag queen-esque, heavily made up middle-aged woman at the coat check and made their way outside to the car park.

"So, your place or mine?" asked Rick, clearly oblivious to Jameson's lack of interest.

"Actually, I think I'm going to call it a night."

"You're kidding right? I paid for dinner and you're just going to go home?" asked Rick, in an increasing agitated tone of voice.

"I'm sorry, I just don't think we're compatible."

"I don't believe this. You're such a fucking cock tease! No wonder your fiancé left you!" shouted the doctor, before storming off to his car leaving Jameson standing speechless in the street.

Jameson was in shock. Firstly, that a grown man – a doctor no less – would act like a petulant toddler and secondly, and most astoundingly, that Rick had been listening long enough to register that Jameson had had a fiancé.

A few moments passed before Jameson sufficiently collected his wits and headed off to his car. While he was glad that he'd managed to escape the clutches of this terrible bore of a man, the experience had also left him feeling lonelier than before. Sadly, all the date had done was drive Jameson's thoughts back to his unobtainable prince who made marvelous coffee.

What if all the good ones really are taken?

Valiantly resisting the urge to buy and devour an obscene amount of ice cream – or call Tom and Finn for some equally as comforting activity – Jameson returned directly home. He planned on sending a tersely worded text to Ruby when he woke up in the morning, although hopefully by then he wouldn't be feeling quite so low.

He crawled into bed, the caress of fresh white cotton sheets comforted him slightly – it was a sensation that he had loved since childhood and it always made him feel safe, secure and loved. Jameson had changed the bed before he went out in the hopes that his date may have gone well.

So much for that!

Jameson switched off his bedside lamp, closed his eyes and slowly drifted off to a dreamless sleep.

* * *

The following morning, Jameson woke up feeling far more hopeful than he had the previous evening. He showered and wandered downstairs for his morning coffee. Through the kitchen window he could see Matt and Trent having breakfast in the sun on the terrace. The duo caught sight of their landlord and waved good morning. Jameson smiled and waved back, once again grateful that he wasn't completely alone.

The espresso machine beeped, letting Jameson know that his fresh fix of caffeine was ready to go. Jameson grabbed his coffee and some fresh fruit and joined the boys outside.

"How was your date?" asked Matt eagerly. The boys had seen him leaving the previous evening all dressed up and had pumped him for information.

"Next question," mumbled Jameson with a grimace.

"Oh well, you just have to kiss a few more toads," remarked Trent in a light-hearted manner.

The trio continued to chat for about twenty minutes or so until the boys needed to leave for their respective shifts at the hotel. Jameson decided to stay on the terrace a little longer, as he liked the feeling of the morning sun on his skin and had nowhere to particularly be. The warmth of the sun soon lulled Jameson into a half-sleeping state. In fact, he undoubtedly would have begun snoring if his phone hadn't started to ring. Jameson sat up with a start, momentarily dazed but quickly regained his bearings. He looked at the display – it was Ruby.

"I hate you," he said into his phone.

"Oh dear, that bad?" asked Ruby.

"Worse!"

"How about lunch? My treat! It's the least I can do," offered Ruby.

"Yes it is, and it better be somewhere expensive…or at the very least have hot waitstaff."

"Of course, dear. I'll pick you up in an hour and you can tell me all the gory details," said Ruby, her voice full of sympathy.

"Don't worry, I'll be letting you know exactly how excruciating it was."

"See you soon, sweetness," drawled Ruby.

A few hours later, the two were headed back to Ruby's car, chatting affably after a scrumptious lunch of pasta and wine down at the pier. They had just walked up the ramp in the parking garage and Ruby was reaching into her handbag for her keys when the pair heard heavy footsteps fast approaching behind them. They turned around to see an irate, burly man barreling towards them.

"You ruined my life you fucking bitch!" yelled the man as he ran at them.

Ruby appeared to recognize the man and automatically assumed a defensive position – self-defense training was an unfortunate necessity in her line of work. Jameson, on the other hand, stood frozen to the spot, not quite sure what to do.

The man continued to charge at them. In a sudden fit of bravery, Jameson moved forward to try and intercept the would-be assailant. Sadly, his heroics were short-lived as the man roughly shoved Jameson to the ground, barely slowing down on his way towards Ruby.

Ruby, however, was apparently far more prepared for the encounter and swiftly stepped out of the way, allowing the attacker's momentum to carry him into a nearby-parked van with a big thud – predictably the man came off second best. He stumbled back to his feet and prepared to charge again but Ruby quickly stopped him in his tracks with a swift knee to the groin followed by one to the face for good measure. He was still yelling obscenities at her while she was straddled across his back securing him with the handcuffs she always kept into her purse...for whenever the need arose.

"Now Keith, isn't it time you calmed down?" asked Ruby, in a sweet voice.

"You filthy whore! I'm going to....ahhhhhh."

The attacker's rant was cut off by Ruby applying pressure to his hands causing the metal edge of the handcuffs to cut into his skin.

"You better call the police," Ruby said to Jameson.

"Right, yeah sure!"

Jameson sheepishly stood up again. He wasn't surprised that Ruby had efficiently dealt with the potentially harmful situation, as she always seemed to have an air of capable confidence about her. Fortunately, there seemed to be no damage to his person, although his ego was more than a little bruised.

"Sorry, I wasn't much help," said Jameson, sounding ashamed.

"Don't be silly. Besides, I'm used to this kind of thing."

While Ruby was apparently taking it all in her stride, Jameson was grateful that none of the cheating men had sought retribution for his part in their downfalls. He reflected that it was a good thing he'd already decided the detective business was most definitely not for him…well outside of a novel at any rate.

Two policemen arrived a few minutes later and couldn't help but laugh when they encountered the scene of a petite Ruby standing with one high heeled foot placed firmly on the back of the husky man on the ground. The man had a bloody nose, which had swelled to twice its size in a matter of minutes and from the look of it he was going to have two black eyes to match.

"She attacked me!" he screamed when the officers came close.

"No, he came at us!" insisted Jameson, feeling the need to defend Ruby given his incompetence during the attack. He also didn't want to look like a wimp in front of the two policemen – particularly the taller of the pair, whose chiseled features, shaved head and solid build set Jameson's mind racing.

"I'm Officer Ford and this is my partner Officer Rayles," said the tall policeman in a deep, resonating voice. "Now, Miss…"

"Washington," responded Ruby, a professional tone creeping into her voice.

"Miss Washington, can you tell me what's going on?"

"The man on the ground is Keith Caruthers and he's the ex-husband of a client of mine."

The policemen looked quizzically at her.

"I'm a private detective," she explained. "His wife hired me to see if he was cheating, which he was…with his secretary. Unfortunately for him, he was also embezzling from his firm to finance the affair – discreet five star hotels and diamond-encrusted trinkets of love don't come cheap," said Ruby, with a knowing smile. "So as you can see he holds a bit of grudge."

"I see. Would you be prepared to come down to the station and make a statement Miss Washington?"

"Ruby, please," purred Ruby in a highly flirtatious manner. "Yes, of course I'll come."

"Would you like me to come too?" asked Jameson.

"Yes, that would be great, Sir," said Officer Ford, while giving Jameson a broad smile.

In that moment Jameson would have gladly followed the officer anywhere he'd asked, although he gently rebuked himself.

He's obviously much more keen on Ruby. Pity…

The policemen bundled a muttering Keith into the back of their squad car and headed off to the precinct with Ruby and Jameson following closely behind in her convertible. They spent the next hour giving their statements and then applying for a restraining order for Ruby. Jameson watched with more than a tinge of jealousy, as Officer Ford appeared to be responding in kind to Ruby's brazen flirtations.

Where's my big, strong knight in shining armor?

Before too long they'd finished all the necessary paperwork and they were headed back to Jameson's townhouse.

"Thanks for an interesting afternoon," said Jameson, when they'd reached his home. "It certainly took my mind off of the disastrous date."

"My pleasure. Maybe we can find a policeman for you next time," teased Ruby, before she drove off.

Or maybe a certain barista…

Jameson smiled ruefully and turned to go inside.

* * *

As Jameson approached his front door he saw a box on the stoop. He was surprised, as he hadn't been expecting anything. There was a familiar logo on the side and Jameson recognized it as belonging to a local florist.

Who'd send me flowers?

Jameson unlocked the door and brought the box inside. He placed it on the kitchen counter and opened it up to find a magnificent bouquet of red roses. After the strange events of the day he was happy to receive this wonderful surprise. That is, until he opened up the card that was taped to the inside of the box and read the inscription.

Dearest Judd,

You are my life, my love, my world. Happy Anniversary Baby!

Love Always, David.

David had apparently given the wrong address when he'd placed his order. Tears streamed down Jameson's face as he slowly sank to the floor. It felt as if his heart had broken into a billion jagged pieces once more. The pain came flooding back inside and it consumed him whole. The sound of his sobbing echoed through the kitchen, as he sat motionless on the floor, the card still in his hand.

The room gradually grew darker as night began to fall, not that Jameson paid any attention. Eventually, when the tears had stopped falling he tried to get to his feet. He only got halfway up before he fell back down to the floor, as his legs were numb. Jameson waited a minute for the circulation to return before trying to stand up again. Once on his feet he made his way to his bedroom, leaving the offending package on the counter. He climbed into bed fully clothed and buried himself under the blankets and covers.

It was here he stayed for the next few days, leaving only to relieve himself or retrieve another bottle of wine from downstairs. Jameson ignored all messages and calls, cutting himself off completely from the world. It seemed as if all the progress he'd made over the last six months had been obliterated by one mistaken delivery. Indeed, he may have sunk completely back into his previous hermit-hood if it hadn't been for his new best friend.

Connor showed up at the townhouse after Jameson had missed two of their regular gym sessions. He knocked on the front door for a while and after receiving no response he went down the side lane of the house and into the backyard. It was then he caught sight of a haggard looking Jameson through the French windows.

Jameson had been ignoring the knocking because he didn't want to face anyone but he no longer had a choice. He unlocked the door and let Connor in.

"What's happened?" asked Connor, his face full of concern.

Jameson simply pointed to the box with the decaying roses inside and walked into the lounge room carrying a freshly opened bottle of rosé. Connor went to the box and saw the card. He immediately pulled out his phone and called Ruby.

"I think you better get over to Jameson's now! He's in a bad way. I'll explain when you get here," said Connor, his wavering voice conveying the urgency of the situation.

"OK, I'll be there in twenty."

Connor then joined Jameson in the lounge room, sitting on the seat beside him.

"Why the fuck does it still hurt so much?" asked Jameson, fresh tears appearing at the corners of his eyes.

"Cause you're human and he's a bastard!"

Connor leaned forward to give Jameson a big comforting hug. They stayed there for quite some time with Jameson crying and sniffling into Connor's shoulder, moving apart only when they heard a knock at the front door.

"Just stay here," insisted Connor.

Not that Jameson had shown much interest in getting up. He waited on the sofa, listening to the murmur of voices as his friends discussed his condition. Jameson was too despondent to object to their intrusion into his solitude, although deep down he was secretly glad not to be alone.

"That stupid piece of…" Ruby's raised voice carried through to the lounge room.

"Oh honey, I'm so sorry," consoled Ruby when she entered with Connor.

They came into the room and sat either side of him. Jameson found their concern touching and was heartened by their friendship.

"OK. No more drinking alone and sulking. Upstairs and get out of those stinky clothes. We're going out!" commanded Ruby.

"I really don't feel up to…" Jameson protested.

"Don't want to hear it! I refuse to let David destroy you all over again. Go, now!"

Jameson turned towards Connor hoping for some support.

"Listen to the lady!" Connor appeared to be in perfect agreement with Ruby.

Reluctantly, Jameson did as he was told and came back downstairs thirty minutes later, freshly shaved and showered, and looking much more like himself. He noticed that the box was gone from the kitchen counter and guessed correctly that his friends had thrown away the disturbing item in his absence.

"So where are you dragging me?" Jameson asked as they headed out the front door.

"Stallions!" cried Ruby, with a mischievous glint in her eye.

"I don't know," said Jameson, feeling rather unsure about going to the well-known male strip club.

"Nothing will cheer you up like cocktails and a lap dance," came Ruby's ready response.

"Damn straight!" Connor chimed in.

Truthfully, the idea of watching hot men gyrating for his pleasure wasn't particularly unappealing. He allowed himself to be led along, knowing full well that if he didn't, he risked turning right back into that depressed, lumpy couch potato of not so long ago.

Who knows, I may actually enjoy myself.

It turned out that an excursion to Stallions was exactly what Jameson needed to break him out of his self-destructive cycle. The trio guzzled down numerous drinks, while rewarding the dancers for their hard work with a stream of dollar bills. All that succulent male flesh made Jameson forget his troubles and by the end of the evening he was floating along on a happy, hazy alcoholic cloud. Connor and

Ruby brought him home and graciously accepted his offer to spend the night – with two guest bedrooms there was plenty of room.

The next morning, Ruby prepared her guaranteed hangover cure for herself and the boys – a delicious breakfast of bacon, eggs and extra-strong black coffee.

Jameson, though bleary-eyed, was feeling better than he had in days. The greasy food and coffee slowly began to work their magic.

"Thank you, guys. I really appreciate what you've done for me," said Jameson, in a most heartfelt manner.

"Any time," responded a smiling Connor.

"You're not getting fat again under my watch," teased Ruby.

The threesome laughed and they continued their breakfast, the mood far lighter than the previous day. Jameson silently promised himself that he wouldn't stop trying to move forward with his life.

I deserve to be happy.

* * *

The next four weeks passed by in a blur, as Jameson threw himself into his writing, only leaving his desk in the attic for meals and quick visits to the gym and beautician – one shouldn't neglect essential maintenance, after all. He had completely immersed himself in the adventures of his great-grandfather and the words flowed freely. All his dedicated work started to pay off and he soon had the manuscript to a point where he was confident in asking Connor and Ruby to have a read through it and offer their opinion. Jameson wanted the book to be as polished as possible before putting his work out into the real world.

"Now, be completely honest," Jameson had instructed the pair, when he'd emailed them their copies.

He knew that the creative world could be a brutal one and it was better if he thickened up his skin with his friends first. There was bound to be lots of rejection and sorrow ahead – it certainly wasn't for the faint of heart – but Jameson figured that he'd already had his feelings stomped on enough so he could handle whatever criticism came his way.

As a reward for finishing his almost-final draft he headed off to Perk Up to treat himself. Jameson hadn't been there for quite some time, as he realized that he would get a lot more done without the distraction of the comely coffee maker. Not to say that Nicolas hadn't crossed his thoughts during those long days of writing but Jameson knew he had to try and move on from his infatuation – although that was easier said than done.

The familiar smell of roasted coffee wafted into his face as Jameson walked into the café.

"Hi, JJ! Have you been away?" asked Nicolas, looking as devilishly handsome as ever.

"No, just been busy with my book." Jameson was quite touched that Nicolas had noticed his absence.

Jameson had told Nicolas all about his planned novel about a month ago. Nicolas had seemed genuinely interested and supportive, as always, and it had only made Jameson want him even more.

"You've got to stop abandoning me, I'm starting to get a complex," said Nicolas, laughing a little.

"Who could ever leave you?"

Stop it! He's taken! Yeah, but he started it. It doesn't matter! But he looks so beautiful. Stop it!

The conflicting thoughts raced through Jameson's head as his heart fought valiantly against his brain. They were alone in the café, the lunch-rush having long finished.

"You want to come here and kiss me?" offered Nicolas.

"I'm sorry...wha...what did you say?" stammered Jameson, more than a bit flustered.

"I said, do you want to try a Honey Pistachio muffin with your tea?" asked Nicolas again. "They're really tasty."

"Sure, that would be good," answered a thoroughly embarrassed Jameson.

Great, now I'm hallucinating!

"So, when can I read it?" asked Nicolas.

"What?"

Jameson was not following the conversation at all.

"Your book."

"I'd prefer to wait until I find an editor and it's all perfect first."

Jameson suddenly felt quite nervous at the prospect of showing Nicolas his work.

"No problem, completely understandable, but I do expect a signed copy," said Nicolas with a cheeky grin.

"Of course," agreed Jameson.

I'd do anything for that smile.

Then completely out of the blue Nicolas added, "Apparently you know my twin sister."

"I do?" asked Jameson, more than a little confused.

"Nora? She works at A Close Shave," explained Nicolas.

Jameson thought about the attractive raven-haired apprentice who'd become his regular nail technician. Now that Nicolas had mentioned it, Jameson could easily see the family resemblance of the full red lips, pale skin and high cheekbones.

"Oh, yes…she's great. My nails have never looked better….How did that come up?" asked Jameson, burning with curiosity.

"It's a little embarrassing. She's always trying to set me up with guys and she talked about this cute client of hers

'Jameson' who was perfect for me. When she described him I knew it must be you," explained Nicolas.

"Doesn't she know you have a boyfriend?" questioned Jameson; ardently hoping that maybe wasn't the case anymore.

"Yeah, but she doesn't really like Sean. Thankfully, it's me dating him not her," chuckled Nicolas.

"Lucky him."

At that moment their eyes locked and Jameson thought he saw a flicker of something more than just pure friendship in Nicolas' gaze.

The barista turned away quickly to put the teapot and cup on the tray and handed Jameson his order.

"Here you go, enjoy!"

Nicolas hurriedly headed off to the storeroom, almost as if he was trying to avoid Jameson. Feeling quite perturbed, Jameson took his order to his usual table and consumed it in silence whilst gazing out the window to the greenery of Janeway Park. His thoughts were even more jumbled than before.

Stop being such a lovesick puppy! What did that look mean? You need to move on!

Jameson knew that he wasn't going to find happiness by pining after someone else's boyfriend but he couldn't deny the strong connection he felt to Nicolas either. After twenty minutes or so of heavy thinking he decided what he needed to do. Jameson gathered his belongings, waved goodbye to Nicolas and headed home to move forward with his new course of action.

5

"OK, I'll do it," said Jameson into the telephone receiver. "But I have some conditions."

"Sure, what do you need?" inquired Connor.

"You and Didier have to come with us and it has to be a daytime thing. The more casual the better," said Jameson firmly.

"I'll have to ask Didier but that should be fine. How does a picnic sound?"

"Perfect. Let me know when it's sorted."

Connor had been pestering Jameson to meet Jacob, a good friend of Didier's, for the past few weeks. For his part, Jameson was hesitant to go on another blind date but he knew that he could only move on from his apparently unrequited crush on Nicolas by putting himself out there in the scary world of dating. This time, however, he made sure that there were safeguards in place to avoid a repeat experience of the dreaded doctor, such as having his friends there to keep things light and casual and thereby take any pressure off.

The foursome met in Janeway Park the following Sunday afternoon. It was a gloriously sunny day and the park was full of fellow Port Davinicans enjoying the summertime. The gentle babble of contented picnickers filled the air. All four had brought along things to eat and drink so they had a veritable feast spread out before them. The conversation flowed freely and Jameson and Jacob seemed to be getting along well.

"You have the most fantastic eyes," remarked an obliviously flirting Jacob.

"Thanks, they run in the family," said Jameson, trying to downplay the compliment.

Physically, Jameson found Jacob rather attractive. He was in his late twenties, had a charming mop of red hair, and a pleasant face with a smattering of freckles across his broad nose. Jacob was slightly shorter than Jameson but had a solid, muscular build that was certainly appealing. The problem was there was just no spark at all. Jameson enjoyed chatting with Jacob but he didn't feel any sort of connection. Part of him couldn't help but wonder if it was because he was unfairly comparing his potential suitor to Nicolas.

"There's a Monet exhibit at the Arnold Gallery if you'd like to go together," suggested Jacob.

"That sounds like fun." Jameson had a sudden pang of conscience, as he didn't want to lead Jacob on. "Just as friends, right?"

"Sure, of course."

Despite his answer, Jacob's bright smile had dimmed ever so slightly and he looked a little disappointed. Jameson looked over at his friends and saw that Connor was affectionately caressing Didier's curly blond locks. They made quite the handsome couple and Jameson couldn't help but feel the familiar twinge of envy whenever he saw a couple in love. He missed having that closeness and companionship, and Jameson couldn't help but wonder if he'd ever have that again.

The boys stayed in the park until the sun started to set and the breeze became just a little too chilly.

"Thanks for a lovely afternoon," said Jameson before he took leave of the others and headed home alone. While saddened he hadn't found a new Prince Charming, Jameson was glad that the date had at least gone far better than the one with Rick.

And I have a new friend.

The thought left him slightly heartened and feeling more positive about the future. Not that he needed a man to complete his life, but who doesn't want to love and be loved in return?

* * *

A few weeks later Jameson's novel – Tea, Scones and a Helping of Murder – was ready, as perfect as it could be in his opinion. He had listened patiently to the suggestions that Connor and Ruby had made, and tried very hard not to take the criticism personally – even though it felt very much like they were insulting his child at times. Jameson had tinkered with the novel, smoothing out the wrinkles in the plot and polishing it as best he could. Now, he was finally feeling confident enough to send his creation off into the world and hopefully to a good home.

After doing a spot of research, he narrowed down the list to around fifty publishers that might be inclined to accept his book. Fortunately, a good many of them only accepted manuscripts via email – better for the environment and good for Jameson's wallet seeing he didn't have to print up and send them all by snail mail. It took him the good part of a day, personalizing his introductory email to all the different publishers and triple checking the name and spelling each time.

By late afternoon he was done and felt proud of himself. He was taking a chance and it felt good. After being cooped up in his study all day, Jameson was definitely in need of some fresh air. He descended the stairs, grabbed his keys and headed out the front door with no particular destination in mind.

Fifteen minutes later he found himself standing in front of Perk Up. Through the glass wall he could see Nicolas behind the counter, fiddling with the espresso machine. Jameson stood there a minute just watching the barista. He was about to walk away when Nicolas suddenly turned around, saw Jameson standing there and waved hello.

Damn it! Can't run away now.

Jameson waved back and went inside. The café was busier than when Jameson normally visited and there was a young girl with blonde dreadlocks and a lip piercing working behind the counter with Nicolas.

"Hi, JJ, the usual?" asked Nicolas.

"Yes, thanks."

"How's the book coming?"

"All done actually," said Jameson, with a touch of pride.

"Seriously? That's fantastic! Your order is on the house, today!"

Nicolas' smile was as wide and inviting as ever.

"No, you don't need to do that," protested Jameson, although he was flattered by the offer.

"Nonsense. You're bound to be a bestselling author and I don't want you to forget the little people," joked Nicolas.

"Oh, I'd never forget you." Jameson said it without thinking.

Dear Lord, did I really just say that?

"Better not, handsome."

Jameson's heart fluttered a little as he took his espresso and Morning Glory muffin went to sit down.

I wonder if he knows what he does to me?

* * *

The following Sunday morning Jameson was on his way out to brunch when he ran into a sheepish-looking Jacob emerging from the side entrance to Matt and Trent's studio apartment. He was obviously a little embarrassed to be caught in a morning walk of shame.

"I didn't know you lived here," he said, apparently very surprised to see Jameson.

They had only seen each other a few times since the picnic, as Jameson always had the feeling that Jacob wanted more from just friendship from him. Jameson was glad to see that Jacob didn't appear to be pining after him.

"Have fun with the boys?" asked Jameson, with a knowing smile.

"Yeah, I was out at Sanctuary last night and ran into those two. I was helpless to resist," joked Jacob.

"Completely understandable."

Indeed, he had seen many a handsome stranger trying to leave discreetly of a weekend morning. His tenants had an open-relationship, something Jameson had found out shortly after they'd moved in together. The promiscuous pair had even offered up their bed to Jameson on a few occasions, which he'd politely refused. Not that he hadn't been tempted at the time, but he'd thought it best not to complicate their tenant/landlord relationship. Besides, by now they were quite good friends and they were more like brothers than potential playmates to him.

"Sorry I've gotta run. I'm catching up with Connor," said Jameson apologetically.

"Say hi for me."

Jacob then headed off down the street, presumably towards home. Jameson hopped in his car and was soon on his way to his and Connor's favorite spot for brunch – One Happy Piggy. His stomach growled and his mouth began to water as his thoughts soon filled with the upcoming culinary delights, especially the white chocolate espresso pancakes...even though he knew full well he'd be spending an extra hour on the treadmill to work them off again.

Beauty is pain!

* * *

Three months had passed since he'd sent out his manuscript and Jameson was becoming doubtful that he'd ever find a publisher. He had received a handful of perfunctory rejection emails – although by their tone he wasn't even sure that they'd bothered to read the book at all. Realistically, he knew that these things did take time but the deafening silence of the publishers who hadn't responded at all gave him cause for concern.

Jameson began to look into the idea of self-publishing on Amazon. It looked a relatively easy process but it wasn't what he really wanted to do. He preferred to have the support of a publisher, both in an editorial and promotional sense.

He had just made himself a strong coffee to kick-start his brain and settled in at his desk to go through his emails when he received a most pleasant surprise. He saw there was a reply from Hastings House, one of the smaller publishing houses he'd applied to. Jameson prepared himself for yet another rejection but as he read the email a smile began to grow upon his face. He read the email again just to make sure he wasn't mistaken, by this time his small smile had become an enormous grin.

It seemed that the owner, Mrs Gwen Hastings, loved his manuscript and wanted to offer him a contract. Wasting no time, he immediately emailed back and within the hour, after a flurry of emails – and the hasty printing, scanning and signing of the contract – he was the newest signed author of Hastings House.

Of course, there was still a great deal of work to be done, before there was a book with his name on it out in the world, but Jameson was so happy he didn't care. As soon as he'd sent off the contract he ran downstairs and banged on the door to Trent and Matt's apartment.

"What's wrong?" asked a bleary-eyed Matt when he finally opened the door. Apparently they'd had yet another big night out.

"Sorry." Jameson felt guilty for waking Matt up but he just had to share his news. "I've just signed with a publisher!" exclaimed Jameson, slightly more loudly than he intended.

The news seemed to wake Matt up slightly.

"That's amazing!" said Matt, while giving Jameson a congratulatory hug. "We should go out tonight and celebrate!"

"I'm planning on it. I'm going to go tell people now."

Jameson was practically vibrating with excitement.

"Just tell us where and when and we'll be there."

"Done. Now go back to sleep. I'll see you guys later."

After Matt closed the door and presumably retreated to the comfort of his bed and boyfriend, Jameson went off to find his phone, still grinning like an overmedicated housewife. In short order he rang Ruby, Connor and then his parents. All of them seemed to be almost as excited as he was at the news.

He made plans to meet up with his merry crew at 8pm that night at The Cat's Meow. There was, however, one person he wanted to invite in person. Half an hour later Jameson walked in the front door of Perk Up. He had only been there once a week of late, as he'd been trying to wean himself off of his infatuation with Nicolas – without much great success. Even so, Jameson wanted to share this momentous news with him.

It was then that Jameson felt a strong surge of disappointment, as it was Prudence, the girl with the blonde dreadlocks, behind the counter instead of Nicolas. He was standing there like an idiot and wondering what to do when he heard someone behind him.

"Hey JJ, you OK? You look kinda lost."

Jameson turned around to face Nicolas, who was carrying a shopping bag full of milk.

"Yeah, I just came by to tell you something but got confused cause you weren't behind the counter," Jameson explained, feeling rather awkward.

"We ran out of milk and I needed to grab some more. I am allowed to leave the café you know." Nicolas was obviously enjoying teasing Jameson. "So?"

"Huh?" asked Jameson.

"You wanted to tell me something?"

"Oh yeah, sorry."

Ergh! What is wrong with me?

"A publisher liked my book and I've just signed with them!" said Jameson proudly.

Without warning Nicolas moved forward and gave Jameson a firm, warm hug...not that he minded.

Mmm...he smells so good.

"Wow! That's awesome! You so deserve it," said Nicolas, still holding the hug.

As much as he was enjoying the close contact, Jameson reluctantly broke away before Nicolas was able to feel exactly how much he liked the hug.

"Anyway, a bunch of us are going out tonight and I stopped by to ask if you'd like to come?" Jameson desperately wanted the barista to say yes. "Sean is invited too, of course," he added, out of politeness.

"I'd love to! But it will be just me. Sean and I broke up a month ago."

"I'm sorry to hear that." Jameson tried his very best to hide his absolute glee at the news.

Could this day get any better?

"I'm sorry, are you OK?" asked Jameson with genuine concern.

"Yeah, it was amicable. It just wasn't working out. We're still friends, so it's all good."

"I'm glad to hear that." Jameson's mind whirled with possibilities. "I gotta go but we'll be at The Cat's Meow round 8."

"Great! I'm looking forward to it."

Jameson left the café and virtually floated home. He booked an appointment at A Close Shave and then pulled out everything in his wardrobe determined to find the perfect outfit. Tonight he wanted to look his very best.

Jameson tried to not let his imagination get too carried away but he couldn't help but be excited by the very real possibility of all his dreams coming true.

* * *

By the time Jameson arrived the bar with Matt and Trent it was already quite busy. They soon found Ruby, Connor and Didier in a booth in the far back corner. He received even more congratulatory hugs and kisses. Jameson was enjoying the extra attention to say the least.

I could get used to this.

Connor went off to the bar to order another round and returned shortly with a delicious array of cocktails.

"To Jameson!" said Ruby, as the group toasted Jameson's success. One cocktail followed another and soon the group was all rather tipsy. Jameson tried to shout a round but his friends refused to let him. While Jameson was enjoying himself, he couldn't help but check the door every five minutes to see whether or not Nicolas had arrived.

"Don't worry, he'll show up," reassured Connor.

The next time Jameson turned to look the entrance he did see someone he knew – Jacob.

"I hope you don't mind I invited Jacob and his new boyfriend along," said Didier, who'd apparently noticed their entrance as well.

"Not at all, the more the merrier."

Even though he appreciated the company of his friends, Jameson was starting to become disheartened.

"Hey guys, this is Andy," said Jacob, introducing the tall, dark-skinned, muscular man by his side.

"Lovely to meet you," said Jameson, glad to have more people to celebrate with and happy that Jacob had found someone special.

Now where's mine?

Jameson did his best to shake all thoughts of Nicolas from his head and enjoy the evening with his friends. He even forced himself to stop anxiously checking the door, which is why he was startled twenty minutes later when he felt a light tap on his shoulder.

"Hi, Sorry I'm so late, we had a plumbing emergency at the café," said Nicolas, apologizing profusely.

"That's so fine!"

Jameson had a grin from ear to ear. He then introduced Nicolas to those at the table he didn't know.

"I'll get the next round," offered Nicolas and soon retreated to the bar.

"Told you," said Connor.

"Damn he's cute, now I know why you're always getting coffee," teased Matt.

"Happy now?" asked Ruby.

"Hush up," Jameson told his laughing friends.

Nicolas soon returned and the toasts began anew. Thirty minutes – and two incredibly strong cocktails – later, Jameson finally decided to bite the bullet. He and Nicolas were standing off to the side from the others chatting, when Jameson, emboldened by the alcohol, uttered the words he'd been dying to say for the last six months.

"So, would you like to go out sometime?" asked Jameson tentatively.

"Aren't we out now?" replied Nicolas, with a cheeky smile.

"No...I mean yes, but..." said Jameson, obviously flustered.

"You're so adorable when you're nervous. I know what you meant." Nicolas leaned forward and planted a gentle kiss on Jameson's lips. "Does that answer your question?".

Jameson immediately kissed him back but with a much stronger intensity, their bodies pressed up against one another.

"Yes," said Jameson. "How about the movies tomorrow night?"

"Actually, I wouldn't mind a private show with you tonight," said Nicolas, with a naughty wink.

"I think that can be arranged."

The very thought of it had Jameson so worked up that he thought the crotch of his jeans may burst open from the force of his straining erection.

"We should probably stay and be social just a little while longer though," added Jameson, conscious of not wanting to abandon his friends.

"That's OK, I'm happy right here."

To illustrate his point Nicolas pressed into Jameson once more. Jameson could easily feel just how happy Nicolas was and couldn't wait until they were alone together. They rejoined the conversation of the others at the table but Jameson could tell from the knowing grins Ruby and Connor were giving him that they had seen all.

After an hour, the bar started to empty out and the group began to disband, saying their goodbyes.

"Don't do anything I wouldn't do," instructed Ruby, which to be frank, gave Jameson license to do pretty much anything.

"I expect a full report tomorrow," whispered Connor, into Jameson's ear.

They shared a cab back to the townhouse with Matt and Trent, who, obviously wanting to give Jameson some privacy, quickly disappeared inside their apartment once they arrived. As soon as Jameson shut the front door behind them Nicolas attacked. He pinned Jameson against the solid wooden door covering him in frantic kisses. The pair pulled at each other's clothing. Shoes, jeans, shirts and underwear all went flying and within minutes they were stripped bare, furiously making out in the foyer.

"I've wanted to do this for so long," gasped Jameson, in between kisses.

"Me too, JJ. I'm all yours," moaned Nicolas in return, as he firmly grasped Jameson's plump buttocks.

Jameson could scarcely believe the moment he'd dreamt of for so long was finally happening. He adored the feeling of Nicolas' lean body pressing him hard up against the door. Their kisses going from soft and tender to hard and passionate, as the two throbbing erections rubbed together, their copious precum leaking and mixing together.

"Bedroom," said Jameson, as he took Nicolas by the hand and led him upstairs. Once there, Jameson pushed

Nicolas onto the bed and began to ravish the barista's body. He kissed Nicolas from his ruby red lips, down his defined chest and rippling six-pack, teasing around the crotch and further down his smooth, toned legs. Jameson then moved back upward until his face was level with Nicolas' manhood. He ran his tongue along the length of the solid shaft, impressed by the thickness and length, until he reached the glistening cock head. Jameson nibbled lightly on Nicolas' chunky foreskin, tugging it gently with his teeth. Above him, Jameson could hear Nicolas groaning in pleasure.

The fingers of Jameson's right hand were wrapped firmly around his playmate's erection, slowly jacking it, as he took Nicolas' cock into his mouth. Jameson's other hand fondled the barista's heavy ball sack, as he began to bob up and down on the delicious dick, taking it deeper into his throat with every downward motion. He could feel Nicolas' hands grasping the back of his head, pulling him in closer.

Jameson breathed in the wonderfully masculine odor as his face pressed into Nicolas' warm crotch. After he'd worked the member for a few minutes, Jameson moved his mouth lower while his hands spread Nicolas' long lean legs. His tongue darted along the skin underneath the balls and into the musky crevice between the globes of Nicolas' firm ass.

"Yeah JJ, just like that," whimpered Nicolas.

Using his hands, Jameson spread Nicolas' legs wider to give him even more access to the hot, tasty hole. Jameson rammed his face in deep, letting his tongue probe the velvety passage. He wanted to taste it all. Jameson ate and ate, relishing every last second of it, as did Nicolas if his moans were any indication.

When he'd had his fill – for the present – Jameson moved back up, kissing Nicolas' smooth, pale skin as he climbed. They soon resumed their passionate kissing, their hands running over increasingly slippery skin…grasping urgently at one another.

A few minutes later, Nicolas broke away and moved down the bed, apparently keen to return the favor. Jameson cried out as he felt the barista's warm mouth engulf his aching cock in one big swallow, expertly deep-throating him – he'd undoubtedly had lots of practice. He gripped Nicolas' shoulders, as the barista swirled and flicked his tongue around and around Jameson's sensitive shaft. A little while passed before Nicolas slid back up to face Jameson and the two kissed once more.

Nicolas reached down and took both the erections in his hand and jacked them together as they continued to kiss. Both boys were so worked up that it only took a few dozen strokes before their climax was at hand. Their breathing became ragged and their sweaty taut bodies tensed up in anticipation. Jameson was first, his load spurting up between the pair and coating their bellies and cocks with his thick cream. Nicolas arrived only a few moments later, adding his own seed to the sticky mess.

They lay back on the bed, holding each other, while their breathing slowly returned to normal and the manly mixture of sweat and semen began to dry on their skin.

Jameson was in heaven. He could have died a happy man right then and there. Fortunately, there was no need for that and the night was far from over.

* * *

Late the following morning, Jameson sleepily rolled over and turned to look at his bedmate, happy to discover that it hadn't all just been a wonderful dream. Nicolas' china blue eyes were open and looking back at him intently.

"Morning, JJ," said Nicolas softly.

"Morning, Nico"

"Nico?" asked Nicolas quizzically.

"You're not the only one you can give nicknames," said Jameson, poking out his tongue.

"Then Nico I am."

Nicolas and Jameson both had contented smiles upon their lips. The pair hadn't gotten much sleep as they been unable to leave each other alone. Jameson had lost count of how many times they'd both cum but it had been enough to make them – and the sheets – rather stiff and sticky.

"Shower?" offered Jameson.

"Lead the way."

Before too long they were wet, soapy and enveloped in the soothing steam.

"So, when can I move in?" asked Nicolas.

"Umm..I...Ummm." Jameson was at a loss for words.

"Just kidding...you're so easy to tease," said Nicolas, as he gave Jameson a quick peck on the lips. "But this better not be a one night stand, Mister."

"Don't worry, I don't plan on letting you go anytime soon."

Jameson pulled Nicolas in towards him for another kiss.

"That's great, cause I've got nowhere else to be," said Nicolas, with a lustful look in his eyes.

Jameson couldn't keep the huge grin off of his face. Unsurprisingly, their efforts at cleaning up led to another bout of play, which only ended when their skin began to prune up. The lusty lads quickly toweled off and headed back to bed to continue their delightful devilment.

6

Over the course of the next month, Jameson was kept busy with editing and cover art decisions, as well as trying to see Nicolas as much as he could. Jameson had only met with Gwen once in person, as most of the communication had been electronic. She was in her late fifties, with kindly blue eyes and a grandmotherly plumpness. Her shiny, chestnut brown hair was always worn up in a chignon. They had developed a good working relationship and Jameson hadn't objected to too many of her suggested changes…she was the professional, after all.

The book was soon ready for release into selected bookshops around Port Davinica, with an initial print run of five hundred copies. Even though Hastings House had their own promotional strategy, Gwen encouraged Jameson to set up his own website to help raise his profile and to promote himself as well as the book.

"Of course, I'd love to do it! It'll probably take a few weeks or so," said Connor, when Jameson had asked for his help.

"Fantastic! What do I owe you?"

"No charge…you just need to keep me in cocktails for the next few months," said Connor, with a cheeky grin.

"Done and done!"

His best friend delivered on his promise and Jameson had a brand new site to help advertise his wares less than a month later. It wasn't just Connor who'd been eager to help. In fact, all of Jameson's close friends were keen to support the fledgling writer by posting links on their various social media platforms. Jameson thought himself extremely lucky to have such wonderfully helpful friends.

Nicolas did his part as well, happily telling all of his regular customers about Jameson's book, clearly proud of his writer boyfriend.

Disappointingly, despite all the enthusiastic support, sales were fairly sluggish for the first month, with only one or two copies being sold in each store and hardly any ebook purchases. Jameson tried not to get discouraged but secretly he had been hoping to be an instant hit with stellar reviews – not that he would admit that to anyone of course.

"Overnight success stories are often years in the making," said Gwen, offering some sage advice.

Realistically, Jameson knew he would have to be patient – not one of his virtues – and concentrate on his next writing project.

One bright spot was that a month after the book's release he received his first piece of fan mail. It had been sent to Hastings House and Gwen had forwarded it on straight away. The letter gushed about Jameson's engaging characters and well-written story. It lifted Jameson's spirits considerably, even though the letter had been unsigned and he had a sneaking suspicion one of his friends had been the one to write it.

Oh well, it's the thought that counts.

* * *

Thankfully, Jameson had a most wonderful distraction to keep him from worrying too much about his less than stellar sales. His blossoming relationship with Nicolas kept Jameson in a near perpetual state of bliss. They hadn't had a talk about making it official but it was clear to anyone who saw them how enamored the pair was with one another.

It hadn't all been perfect though. At the start, Jameson had had a niggling doubt that the real-life Nicolas may not be able to compete with the fantasy version he'd created in his head. Fortunately, his concern was unfounded as Nicolas easily lived up to expectation. He was just as thoughtful, kind and loving as Jameson had dreamed he would be. Then there was the sex, which only seemed to get better as they became more familiar with one another's bodies. Certainly, there wasn't a square inch of each other they had hadn't explored and played with fully. They fit perfectly...in oh so many combinations.

Jameson generally avoiding going into Perk Up these days, as he knew he wouldn't be able to keep his hands off of Nicolas – and vice versa. Indeed, the last time he'd been there they'd been unable to resist their natural urges and had had a very frantic session in the storeroom. While it had been enjoyable, it wasn't very professional and Jameson didn't want to get Nicolas in trouble, even if he was the manager. They saw each other most days and had managed to defile every room in both Nicolas' apartment and Jameson's townhouse. They were fornicating at a rate that even rabbits would baulk at.

It would be fair to say that Nicolas was the best lover he'd ever had, which was saying something given the amount of men Jameson had had in his time. Not to say he'd been a complete slut but he wasn't exactly a stranger to the delights of a friendly orgy...or several.

Happily, their non-carnal time was just as pleasurable. They talked for hours, about everything and anything. It was during one of these engaging chats that Jameson learnt something altogether surprising about his paramour. They were lying together in a hammock, which was strung up between the two sturdy oak trees in Jameson's garden. Clad only in shorts, as the day was hot, their bare skin was slick with perspiration, despite the gentle breeze.

"Your dad is a priest?!?" asked Jameson, not quite believing what his boyfriend had just told him.

"Yep. Father Paul. Well he was a priest, until he met my mother that is." Nicolas had a mischievous twinkle in his eye. "He used to teach at Saint Francis Xavier, then he had a secret affair with one of the parishioners, which caused a bit of a scandal as you'd well imagine. Of course, they were shunned, particularly when it came out that my mum was expecting. So, they ran away to Canada and had me and Nora," explained Nicolas matter-of-factly.

"So you're a divine gift?" teased Jameson.

"Something like that."

Nicolas gave his boyfriend's nipple a sudden tweak. Jameson yelped and the hammock rocked violently.

"What was that for?" demanded Jameson.

"You loved it!"

"That's beside the point," said Jameson, in a fake huff.

Nicolas bent forward and lightly kissed the assaulted nipple.

"Better?" he asked gently.

"Much."

Nicolas went on to explain that while his parents had remained relatively religious, they had been nothing but supportive and loving towards him when he'd revealed his preference for men.

"Besides, it's hardy like they were in a position to judge, given their history," said Nicolas.

"I was pretty lucky with my family too. My parents were more concerned with good grades than who I was dating, although they did so hope I'd marry a doctor," joked Jameson.

"Do you think they'd settle for an underwear model?" asked Nicolas, in a semi-serious tone.

"Why are you proposing?"

Jameson was enjoying the game they were playing.

"Not yet…but Nicolas Nightingale-James has a nice ring to it, don't you think?" said Nicolas, giving Jameson an affectionate kiss on the forehead.

"Maybe your dad could marry us?" suggested Jameson, smirking.

"Sure why not."

Jameson snuggled into Nicolas further, feeling as content as he'd ever been, as the light summer breeze caressed their entwined bodies.

* * *

After another month of poor sales, Gwen organized a series of in-store appearances, where Jameson would read a small passage from his book and sign copies afterwards.

"Now don't get discouraged if there aren't too many people," counseled Gwen, in an apparent effort to keep Jameson in a positive frame of mind.

"I'll be happy if anyone shows up at all," remarked Jameson, trying to downplay the growing worry he felt that he was a terrible writer and no one else would want to buy his book.

The first two bookshops only had ten people in the audience and half of those were people he knew. Admittedly, it did help to see the friendly faces of Connor and Ruby each time, and, of course, the handsome features of his boyfriend watching him lovingly.

It was at the third store, however, where things seemed to be changing. The Pink Page was located near the center of the gayborhood and still did a roaring trade despite the popularity of online book sales. The assembled crowd was more than the previous two combined and Jameson didn't recognize most of them.

After he'd finished reading the applause seemed more enthusiastic than his other appearances, possibly because he'd chosen one of the more racy passages this time. Afterwards, people lined up in an orderly queue by the small desk that they'd set up, for them to meet Jameson and have him sign their copies.

While all those in line were complimentary about his novel, some were exceeding generous in their praise, in particular a rotund middle-aged lady by the name of Anne Chalmers.

"I've read it three times already. I just love Sébastien and Flynn! You write so well!" gushed Anne.

"Thank you very much." Jameson replied with a great deal of modestly.

"I've told all my girlfriends to buy and read it! I can't wait for your next one!" Anne seemed to get even more excited as she spoke. "You're my new favorite author!"

"That's wonderful to hear."

Jameson was certainly flattered by the attention. It was then Gwen discreetly swooped in, in an attempt to keep the queue moving at a constant pace. Jameson kept signing and chatting with his new fans for the next hour. He was pleasantly surprised to see the last person in the queue was someone else he knew.

"Hey! Connor told me about the reading, so I thought I'd check it out. That bit you read was really hot, can't wait to read the rest," said Jacob.

"Hi, I didn't see you before. Glad you enjoyed it. How's Andy?"

"He's well. Anyway, it was good to see you. I've got to head to work. Catch you soon."

"Thanks for coming!" said Jameson, genuinely glad of the support.

Jameson had just begun to pack up the chairs when Nicolas came up and gave him a quick peck on the lips.

"Connor and Ruby have just gone next door to grab some coffees but they'll be back in a sec. It seemed to go really well today, I'm so proud of you, JJ."

Just then Gwen came up with a big, warm smile.

"Good news, they've sold out!" said Gwen.

"Really? That's great!" said a pleasantly surprised Jameson.

"Yes, indeed. The manager has already ordered in more copies and hopefully the next two readings will go just as well," said Gwen, exuding positivity.

"Fame and fortune here I come!" Jameson said laughingly.

Before too long they'd finished tidying up and they rejoined Ruby and Connor in the street. They decided to walk back to Jameson's townhouse seeing it was only five blocks away and it was a lovely evening. Jameson was unlocking the front door when he froze. There on the doormat was a single red rose. He hadn't seen it straight away, as it was nearly dark. Jameson slowly bent down to pick it up.

"Who's it from?" asked Nicolas.

"I don't know, there's no note."

It can't be David.

"Maybe you have a secret admirer?" said Ruby.

"Or a crazed fan?" added Connor.

"Well you're nobody until you have a stalker," Jameson joked, although he was a little concerned.

"As long as they know you're all mine," said Nicolas, grabbing Jameson in a big bear hug and nuzzled his neck.

"I think everyone knows that," remarked Ruby with mock exasperation.

"For sure," added Connor.

"OK, OK, enough of all that," said Jameson, as he unlocked the door. "Time for some wine!"

"No arguments here," said Ruby.

The foursome trundled inside and the spent the rest of the evening toasting Jameson's burgeoning success.

* * *

The following Saturday saw Jameson standing in a bedroom watching seven boys in their underwear having a pillow fight on a king-sized bed. It was a thoroughly camp and deliciously homoerotic display.

He wasn't alone, as there were six other people in the room watching the proceedings with great interest. Jameson was on the set of the latest CocKed underwear photo shoot and he was happily watching his boyfriend, pose, play and pout for the camera.

The bedroom in question belonged to one of the other models – Thad – a bronzed blond twink, who lived with his boyfriend, Simon, in the suburbs of Port Davinica. Their spacious home had been chosen for the location due to the accommodating size of the bed – it had certainly hosted quite a few men in its time – and for the large pool in the backyard. The plan for the day was to capture the group 'slumber party' in the morning and shoot some poolside antics in the afternoon, to show off the new swimwear range when the natural lighting was better.

Jameson had eagerly accepted Nicolas' invitation to come watch. He had been ogling the CocKed posters for the last year so he was keen to see how they were made...and the idea of watching underwear models frolic was pretty much every red blooded male's fantasy. Earlier in the day, Nicolas had proudly introduced his boyfriend to the other models. It was strange to see the boys, whose bodies he knew so well, live in the flesh, although Jameson had already met the stunning, ebony-skinned Gabriel, who also happened to be the assistant manager at Sweat Station...such a small world at times.

The photographer, Spencer, a handsome brunette in his mid-thirties, capably ordered the boys around, positioning them to show off their assets in the best possible way. Jameson was standing off to the side with Simon, watching the boys hard at work. They chatted quietly as Spencer's camera clicked away.

"You must be proud of Thad," said Jameson.

"Yeah, my boy is beautiful." Simon responded with a touch of smugness. Not that Jameson could begrudge him that, as he felt the exact same way about Nicolas.

"Is it weird seeing your brother and your boyfriend playing around up there like that?" asked Jameson.

Simon's brother, Ali, had been recently added to the CocKed lineup, along with James, a former marine turned personal trainer. Both men were strapping specimens of manhood, Ali's swarthy and hairy muscular build contrasted well with James' smooth fairer complexion. And both fit in well with the others, who were eclectic mix of tantalizing skin tones and builds. The new campaign revolved around the days of the week seeing they had seven models, with a highly suggestive tagline – Get CocKed Daily!

"No, it's all in good fun." Simon was quick to reply, although his eyes didn't seem to say the same thing.

It gave Jameson pause for thought, as he watched Spencer's assistant, Angela, a tattooed lesbian with smoky eyes and short platinum hair, re-apply makeup where the boys had rubbed it off each other with their roughhousing.

How flirty and touchy Nicolas seemed to be with the other models started to make Jameson feel uneasy.

Should I be jealous?

"Enjoying the show?" asked Nicolas, when they had broken for a light lunch – no one wants to see bloated models.

"Yes, very entertaining, indeed." Jameson gave his boyfriend an affectionate pat on the butt. He tried to ignore the little voice in his head that suggested Nicolas was enjoying himself a little too much.

Jameson's demeanor didn't improve as the boys changed into their swimwear and moved onto the second setting. The shots started innocently enough with the boys lazing by the pool in the sun and splashing each other. Things soon became racier, however, when encouraged by Spencer, the boys began pulling at each other's swimwear, causing buttocks to be bared and crotches to swell – a perfectly natural reaction to such manly play.

Jameson's thoughts took a slightly darker turn when he saw how well Ali and Nicolas were getting along together and how often they seemed to be rubbing up against each other in the pool.

How long until they're sleeping together?

Jameson continued to watch the boys frolic for another twenty minutes or so until it was time for individual shots. All the boys, except James, climbed out of the pool and toweled off and lazed in the sun lounges by the side of the pool, until it was time for their shot. Nicolas came over and sat down by Jameson, beads of water still trickling down from his hair and onto his smooth, defined chest.

"Everything OK?" asked Nicolas, apparently noticing the worried look on Jameson's face.

"Yeah, I'm just a little tired." said Jameson, lying to Nicolas for the first time.

Just talk to him!

Unfortunately, Jameson was reluctant to bring up his jealousy and fear of betrayal…just yet. Nicolas gave Jameson a warm kiss on the lips and put his arm around him.

"I'm so glad you're here."

Nicolas snuggled his still wet body against his boyfriend. Jameson's jealousy quickly faded and he felt like an absolute idiot. He had built up an entire scenario in his head that had no basis in fact and everything to do with his own over-sized, emotional baggage.

"Me too."

Jameson pulled Nicolas in closer and gave him a loving kiss in return.

Just wait' till my therapist hears about this.

* * *

Unbeknownst to everyone, Jameson had been seeing a therapist once a week for months. Even with as much progress as he'd made moving on with his life, Jameson had realized he could still benefit from a spot of professional help. His friends were great and amazingly supportive but he thought he needed an objective voice to help him sort through his issues.

Doctor Evelyn Waters was in her early sixties, with wavy, gray hair cascading over her shoulders, a suspiciously line-free face and a penchant for pantsuits. Overall, she possessed a commanding presence that Jameson found comforting. Their sessions had been quite cathartic and he felt like he was making real progress.

"So, why didn't you use it as an opportunity to discuss you trust issues? He does know about David and Judd, after all," asked Dr. Waters.

Her shrewd blue eyes seemed to be looking right inside Jameson's heart.

"It wasn't the right time," explained Jameson. "He was working and…"

"Piss posh!" interjected Dr. Waters.

She had a habit of calling Jameson out whenever she suspected that he was holding back the truth.

"OK, I was frightened. I didn't want to scare him off with how damaged I really am," said Jameson, self-consciously.

"Well, if you want this relationship to work you need to be honest about your feelings. Otherwise, these issues will continue to eat away at the foundation of your relationship until there is nothing left for it to stand on."

As much as the prospect of having a discussion with Nicolas about his issues terrified Jameson, he knew that the good doctor was right.

"So, when you come back next week, I want to hear that you've at least broached the subject with Nicolas. From what you tell me he sounds like a wonderfully understanding lad and you're doing him a disservice by not putting your faith in what you have together."

Harsh, but fair.

"OK, I will," promised Jameson, with a resigned air.

Sadly, it was a promise that Jameson would be unable to keep.

7

"I wish I was going with you," said Jameson over the phone.

"Me too, but it's not a good time. I'll message you when we get there," said Nicolas, his voice tinged with sadness.

"Fly safe, Nico."

Jameson put down his phone and looked forlornly into his rapidly cooling coffee, wishing he wasn't going to be separated from his boyfriend.

The previous evening, he and Nicolas had been watching television on the sofa in Nicolas' apartment when they'd received some distressing news. Nicolas' father had been involved in a serious accident. Apparently, Paul Nightingale had been out for his usual afternoon run when a car had struck him down. The driver, an elderly woman, had had a heart attack and crashed up onto the footpath.

Fortunately, a doctor had been driving by and had stopped to help. Nicolas' father had broken bones and internal bleeding but had been moved from a critical to stable condition overnight. Sadly, the driver wasn't as fortunate and passed away at the scene.

Naturally, Jameson had offered to go with Nicolas to comfort him in his time of need but had understood when his boyfriend had said no. Besides, it wasn't exactly how he wanted to meet Nicolas' parents for the first time.

Over the next few days they spoke at least twice a day and texted each other like lovesick teenagers. It appeared that they were equally as upset by the unexpected separation. This didn't stop Jameson from becoming more than a little jealous when he received Nicolas' latest message, which included a picture he sneakily taken of the smoking hot doctor treating his father.

He's probably already taken Nicolas' temperature! Stop it now! Why are you looking for problems? I don't want to lose him.

Jameson's troubled mind turned on itself and left him feeling out of sorts. Realistically, he knew Nicolas had never given him any cause for concern and that the betrayal only existed in his overactive imagination. He resolved to talk to Nicolas about it when his boyfriend got back to town.

That afternoon, when Jameson got back from the gym there was a small package waiting on his stoop – an exquisitely wrapped box of Swiss chocolates. There was no note attached.

First the rose, now this? Apparently I have a secret admirer.

When Ruby came over later that evening for dinner he told her about the chocolates.

"You should be careful that you don't have a stalker, these things tend to end badly," Ruby advised him.

"Please, I'm nowhere near interesting enough for that," said Jameson self-depreciatingly.

It did unsettle him though, that both presents had been left anonymously on his doorstep.

How do they know where I live?

"Here, why don't you take the number for my self-defense classes," said Ruby, as she handed Jameson a card for the Golden Tiger Center.

"Sure, it can't hurt to give it a go. Anyway, have a chocolate. They're delicious, no matter who sent them," said Jameson, popping a fifth one in his mouth.

Ruby took one and soon agreed with his assessment.

"Urgh, that'll be an extra spin class this week," complained Ruby.

"For you and me both, my dear," commiserated Jameson.

* * *

Nicolas returned at the end of the next week, as his father had been released from hospital and was doing well. The boys had a most enjoyable and rather sweaty reunion, which lasted well into the night. The following day the loved-up couple were enjoying a lunch of spicy mixed enchiladas, on the terrace of The Flaming Sombrero with Connor and Didier, when a most unexpected event occurred.

"Jameson!" called a female voice.

Jameson turned around and saw that it was the enthusiastic lady from his book signing, accompanied by two similarly plump middle-aged women.

"Do you remember me? It's Anne. I was walking by with my friends and I just had to say hello. I've been telling my friends all about your book and they've bought copies as well. Excuse my manners, this is Deidre and Beth. They just love your book too!" gushed Anne.

She appeared even more excited than the last time Jameson had met her – if that was even possible. Anne's face was a little flushed and she looked as if she might try and lean in for a hug. The other diners on the terrace had turned to look at Jameson, apparently eager to see who this celebrity was among their midst.

"Pleased to meet you," said Jameson, to Anne's friends. His politeness overcame his embarrassment over the fuss Anne was making.

"I'm so sorry to have disturbed your lunch. We'll go now, but it was so wonderful to see you again!" Anne then swiftly departed with her friends in tow.

"See I told you he was handsome and so polite…."

Anne's voice faded as the trio continued down the street.

"Maybe she's your secret admirer!" teased Connor.

"You better keep an eye on him," added Didier.

"Should I be worried," asked Nicolas, barely keeping a straight face.

"You guys are hilarious, too funny," said Jameson, sarcasm dripping from his words.

"You're a celebrity now, you'll have the paparazzi following you next!" said Connor, in a slightly mocking manner.

"No photos please! Mr James needs his privacy!" joked Didier.

Jameson took the good-natured ribbing in his stride. After all, such attention was only bound to increase if his books continued to sell.

Oh well, it's a sacrifice I'm willing to make.

* * *

A few weekends later Jameson and Nicolas found themselves headed to Sanctuary for the launch of the new CocKed campaign, which was in the form of an underwear party…it was one of the hottest tickets in town. As was the custom with all their promotional events, all the models – and their playmate of choice – were given free samples of the latest designs to help display them on the night – what better way to show off their wares, after all?

Due to Nicolas being one of the 'stars' of the evening, he and Jameson were able to skip straight past the queue and enter through the VIP entrance. Nicolas also had a fistful of drink vouchers, as did all the magnificent models, thanks to the generosity of the management of Sanctuary.

By the time Jameson and Nicolas arrived, the place was already filling up with a wide variety of men – twinks, daddies and everything in between…something for everyone really. Loud music pounded through the club as the revelers drank, danced and generally enjoyed themselves as they frolicked about in their underwear.

Partygoers were encouraged to get their photos taken with the models and even had the opportunity to purchase the new underwear range right there and then. Also, to help keep the crowd entertained, muscular gogos were positioned on each of the five podiums, teasing the crowd with their almost hypnotic gyrations.

Jameson and Nicolas had been there for a few hours, and were on their sixth round of Mojitos, when Jameson suddenly spotted two men that he'd only ever seen on screen – namely his favorite porn stars Brady Summers and Cody Fox. To be honest, he hadn't actually watched one of their scenes in quite a while now seeing his needs were more than being met by his beautiful boyfriend, but it didn't stop him from feeling like a shy schoolboy.

"Do want to meet them?" asked Nicolas, after he noticed where Jameson was staring.

"Oh no, I wouldn't want to disturb them."

Jameson was feeling strangely timid.

"It's no problem, I've already met them a few times. Their studio has a deal with CocKed."

Now he thought about it, they did always seem to be wearing CocKed underwear, albeit briefly, in their films.

"Are you sure?" asked Jameson.

"Come on fanboy," teased Nicolas.

They moved over to where the two porn stars were standing by the side of the main dance floor.

"Hi guys! Having a good night?" said Nicolas, raising his voice to be heard over the music.

"Hey Nicolas, yeah we are," replied Cody.

"This is my boyfriend, Jameson. He's a big fan!" said Nicolas, giving his boyfriend a good-natured grin.

Jameson gave him a playful slap on the arm.

"Nice to meet you," said Brady.

"Always a pleasure to meet an admirer," added Cody with a lascivious wink.

"You guys do beautiful work," gushed Jameson, hoping he didn't sound too much like a crazed fan.

"Thanks, we try our best," said Cody laughing.

The boys were just as stunning in person as they were on the screen, and both were wearing the skimpiest jockstraps, which bordered on indecent. Jameson barely knew where to look. He felt completely star-struck...he suddenly had a lot more sympathy for Anne.

Just then, a tall attractive redhead with cute dimples interrupted them. It was Adam, the creative director, and co-owner, of CocKed Inc, who Jameson had met during the photo shoot.

"Sorry, but I need to borrow Nicolas for a little bit," said Adam.

He was rounding the models up for yet another series of group shots.

"Don't worry we'll look after Jameson for you," offered Brady, with a mischievous glint in his eyes.

"Just don't give him back too soiled," replied Nicolas, with a laugh.

He gave Jameson a quick peck on the mouth.

"I won't be long, JJ," said Nicolas, before disappearing off into the crowd.

"Come on let's dance," commanded Cody, grabbing Jameson by the hand.

Jameson didn't have a chance to object, as Cody led him towards the middle of the crowded dance floor, with Brady following closely behind him, sliding past the sweaty muscular backs and chests of their fellow dancers. The heady aroma of masculine exertion seemed to engulf them as they moved further and further in.

Not that Jameson was opposed to being dragged along, as he'd long fantasized about such an encounter. Indeed, thoughts of these two strapping men had seen him through some very dark moments after the breakup with David.

Before he knew it, Jameson was sandwiched between the couple, their slick, barely-clad bodies pressed firmly up against him as they ground together. Jameson felt slightly guilty but soon lust was the only thing in his mind as he felt two rapidly hardening cocks poking into him. Cody was in front of him and looking down Jameson saw that the porn star's monstrous manhood was threatening to escape, the glistening cock head peeking over the waistband of the jockstrap. Behind him, Jameson felt Brady's equally impressive inches rubbing into the crease of his buttocks. His own cock stiffened in response…how could it not? He felt the hands of both Cody and Brady exploring his body – grabbing, tweaking and scratching – and Jameson's hands were soon reciprocating in kind. Their mouths expertly nibbled on Jameson's neck and shoulders, sending little electric shocks of pleasure through his body. He was in heaven, his fantasy come to life. It was then that reality set in when he happened to turn his head to side and saw Nicolas looking right at him, from a raised platform near the side of the dance floor.

Suddenly, Jameson was flooded with guilt and despair. He had been so jealous of Nicolas' imaginary hi-jinks with his fellow models and here Jameson was doing far worse. He quickly broke away from the pair and made his way up to his boyfriend.

"I'm so sorry Nico," said Jameson, almost on the verge of tears.

"For what? Are you OK?"

Nicolas' face was the very picture of confusion. He took Jameson by the hand and led him further off to the side where it was a little less noisy.

"For the way I was acting with the guys," explained Jameson, with an expression full of shame.

"Seriously? You were just playing. It's not like you were full-on fucking them."

"Yeah but I wanted to."

Misery was written all over Jameson's face.

"So? So would I. They're damn hot!".

"You're not mad?" asked Jameson, thoroughly confused.

"About a little bit of dirty dancing? I think you need to give me a bit more credit than that."

Nicolas was apparently more put out by Jameson's assumptions than his actions.

"I thought I'd ruined everything!"

"Listen JJ, you're not going to lose me over a harmless bit of fun. Besides we haven't even talked about being monogamous."

"I've been such an idiot. I was worried that you'd been playing around and that I'm not good enough to deserve you."

The words that he'd been blocking up came tumbling out in a rush, as he confessed his fears. He knew that this was a conversation he should have had with Nicolas in a nice private setting with a glass of wine, instead in the middle of a crowded nightclub.

"Of course, you'd have trust and jealousy issues after what you've been through. It's only natural," said Nicolas, in a reassuring tone.

"I don't want anyone but you," proclaimed Jameson.

"Neither do I."

"You sure?" asked Jameson timidly.

Nicolas leaned forward and gave Jameson a hard, passionate kiss.

"Let's get out of here and I'll show you just how sure I am," said Nicolas, his eyes full of mischief.

"You don't need to stay?" Jameson didn't want his insecurities to affect Nicolas' career.

"Nah, that was the last lot of photos. I'm all yours, my love." Nicolas gave Jameson another reassuring kiss.

"I should probably apologize to the guys for leaving so abruptly," said Jameson, in a funny show of politesse.

"I think they'll get over it," said Nicolas, gesturing over to Cody and Brady who already had another lad happily writhing between them.

Jameson took Nicolas by the hand and led him out of the club, a wide smile plastered on his face. They jumped into a cab back to Jameson's townhouse and spent the night making sweet, tender love until they were both well and truly exhausted.

* * *

On a Friday night, a few weeks later, Jameson was cuddled up on the sofa with Nicolas watching Breakfast at Tiffany's – who can resist Audrey in a tiara? It felt ever so warm and comfortable.

Ever since their conversation at Sanctuary, Jameson felt a new sense of calm and contentment. He wasn't foolish enough to think that all of his emotional hang-ups had disappeared but he had renewed faith in Nicolas, their relationship and, most importantly, himself.

They were spending so much time together that they were practically living together. Not that Jameson was quite ready to take that big step just yet, although he had given Nicolas a key. They had only been officially together for four months – even if it did feel like much longer.

It had been strange at first having Nicolas there, especially with all the memories of David about the place, but Jameson had grown quite used to having him around. Matt and Trent also seemed to approve of the new semi-landlord, the foursome often enjoying breakfast on the terrace together.

"Did you borrow my green converses?" asked Jameson.

Despite being different clothing sizes their feet matched perfectly.

"Nope, haven't seen them."

"That's weird I haven't worn them in a while."

Jameson was puzzled at their disappearance.

"Maybe the poltergeist took them?" suggested Nicolas, with a grin.

It was their little in-joke. Over the past few months little things had been going missing – the paperweight from his desk, pairs of underwear, his favorite dildo – only to turn up in odd places later on. It had happened so often that they had decided it must be a restless gay ghost looking for a bit of fun.

"I'm sure they'll turn up," said Jameson, nuzzling into Nicolas' neck.

Damn! How does he always smell so good?

They enjoyed the rest of the film, cozily wrapped up together, before taking themselves off to the bedroom for some serious snuggling.

8

Jameson was exiting Dr. Water's office after his regular Wednesday session, looking at his phone and not paying attention to where he was going and he ran straight into someone.

"I'm so sorry, I …" Jameson began, stopping when he recognized Jacob. "Oh, what are you doing here?"

"I have an appointment," said Jacob, sounding defensive.

"I'm sorry, that was terribly rude of me. I just wasn't expecting to see anyone I know," said Jameson apologetically, after remembering his manners.

"That's OK. Some people can be funny when they find out you're in therapy. Dr. Waters is great! She's really helped me through some tough times. How are you anyway? How's Nicolas?"

"Good, he's good too. In fact we're off to the mountains this weekend for a romantic getaway."

"That sounds wonderful. I should go. I don't want to be late for my session. Have a great weekend!"

"I'm sure we will…if we aren't eaten by bears," Jameson joked. "You have a good weekend too."

Jameson left the office building and continued onwards to the gym where he was due to meet Connor for a weights session and stretch class. Admittedly, he had felt a little embarrassed seeing Jacob but quickly realized that he was being foolish. Jameson knew he still worried too much what people thought of him. Ironically, it was one of things he had been working on with Dr. Waters.

Why does it matter if people know? Oh well, guess I'm still a work in progress.

He smiled at the thought as he walked, enjoying the warm evening air as he made his way to the gym.

* * *

After three hours cooped up in the car, Nicolas and Jameson were glad to finally arrive at their destination. The last few miles seemed to take forever, as they'd been driving along a narrow winding dirt road, but Jameson knew it was well worth the journey. It had been Jameson's idea to go camping there as he had many pleasant memories of similar trips with his parents and brother when he was little. Sadly, he hadn't been in quite some years as David's idea of roughing it had been a three star hotel. Yet another way they'd been thoroughly unsuited.

They had pulled up just outside the ranger's cabin – a rustic-looking wooden building set in a small clearing. The door soon opened and a large lumberjack of a man came out to greet them. The light green ranger uniform clung to his imposing frame and showed off taut tanned muscles born from manual labor in the great outdoors. The boys both did their best to not openly stare at the strapping specimen before them – they may be blindly in love but some sights were impossible to ignore.

"Hi, I'm Ranger Davies, but you can call me Isaac. Welcome to Christie National Park. You folks here for the weekend?" asked the ranger.

"Yes. I'm Jameson and this is Nicolas. We were planning on camping down by the small lake in the next valley. I used to go there all the time as a kid."

"Ah yes, that's one of my favorite spots. You're lucky too, there are hardly any other campers in the park this weekend, so you should have the place pretty much to yourselves."

This was pleasing news to Jameson, as he'd been looking forward to enjoying the full splendor beauty of nature by indulging in all manner of unnatural acts with his boyfriend…something he didn't feel inclined to share with the ranger.

They said goodbye to Isaac and drove along the road – or rather dirt track by this point – over the ridge and down to the lake.

"Damn, you weren't kidding!" exclaimed Nicolas, when he stepped out of the car and looked around.

The lake was situated fairly high up in the mountains and had stunning views back down the valley and eastward to the ocean. All around the clearing there were wildflowers, seemingly in ever color imaginable. The woods surrounding the area were quite thick but there were a few trails where one could hike and commune with nature. The crisp mountain air made a refreshing change from the city pollution.

They unloaded the equipment at a leisurely place and had the tent set up and ready for habitation, without too much trouble. Jameson had a quick scout around the nearby trees and soon had an ample supply of firewood to see them through the weekend.

The day was hot and the crystal clear water of the lake began to look rather inviting.

"Fancy a skinny dip?" asked Jameson, giving Nico a suggestive wink.

"Sure, I'm game."

The duo stripped off and raced each other to the water. They splashed in, the cool water tingling on their exposed flesh.

"It's colder than I thought it would be," said Nicolas, shivering a little.

"Want me to warm you up?" asked Jameson, with a wayward glint in his eyes, as he moved towards Nicolas.

"I wouldn't be opposed to it."

Nicolas opened his arms wide. The twosome came together their naked bodies entwining, as they began to kiss slowly. Unsurprisingly, their manhoods were soon engorged and ready for action. The lovebirds were in no rush, however, and were content to simply float in the water as their tongues swirled around and around inside each other's mouths.

They were so caught up in the moment that they hadn't head the approach of another vehicle. Indeed, they remained oblivious to the presence of someone watching them until a deep, manly voice boomed across the lake.

"Hi guys, sorry to interrupt you," said Isaac, although he didn't look too unhappy to have come upon the very erotic scene.

Jameson and Nicolas jumped apart at the unexpected intrusion and instinctively put their hands down to cover their extremely noticeable erections. A little too late given that the ranger was only standing about fifteen feet away on the bank of the lake and had seen pretty much everything.

"I've just heard on the weather service that there's a good chance of a nasty storm front headed this way tomorrow. It may pass us by but it's best to be prepared," warned Isaac.

"Thanks for that," said Jameson, feeling slightly mortified at being caught.

"Yeah, thanks," added Nicolas, who seemed to be equally embarrassed.

"Well I'll let you get back to it." Isaac gave them a cheeky grin. "You boys have fun now."

Isaac climbed back into his 4WD and left the boys in peace.

"I can't believe he caught us, although he was pretty cool about it," said Nicolas, still feeling the heat of embarrassment.

"He probably wanted to join in," joked Nicolas. "Should we worry about the weather you think?"

"We'll just keep an eye out and I'm sure Isaac would come back and tell us if we were in any danger."

"I'd protect you from the ravages of nature!" said Nicolas, with a mock air of bravado.

"My hero."

Jameson kissed Nicolas on the forehead. Nicolas kissed Jameson back on the mouth with a sudden urgency.

"I want you," said Nicolas, with a hungry look in his eyes.

"I'm all yours, Nico."

Their bodies pressed together, sliding over each other, the sun tan lotion they'd applied earlier made them slippery as eels. Nicolas moved his hands downward and gripped Jameson's firm buttocks in his large hands. He spread them wide and then inched his fingers into towards the sensitive, exposed hole.

Jameson felt the thick digits poking at his entrance and tilted his hips back to give his boyfriend easier access. First one, then another, finger worked its way inside causing him to gasp in pleasure while Nicolas lightly bit Jameson's neck. Nicolas teased Jameson's hole, running the fingers in circular motions, pushing in deeper then withdrawing nearly all the way out. After ten minutes of such exquisite torture Jameson was groaning almost constantly.

"Please fuck me," he whispered into Nicolas' ear, when he could take the anticipation no longer.

Nicolas moved the two of them closer to the side and half-lay Jameson down on the muddy bank of the lake. He spread Jameson's thighs wide apart and moved between them, positioning his thick cock head against his boyfriend's rosebud. Nicolas leaned forward to kiss Jameson deeply as he began to push against the tight entrance. The water and the slickness of the oil barely provided enough lubrication, so Nicolas took his time working his solid eight inches into the awfully snug passage. Neither was in a rush, they had nowhere to be other than each other's arms. Nicolas pushed and ground his way inside and was soon rewarded with the smooth globes of Jameson's buttocks pressed firmly against his crotch. Then Nicolas began to make love to his bronzed beau with slow, steady thrusts.

Jameson writhed in the mud as each poke of his prostate sent a wave of pleasure through his entire body. He loved the feeling of Nicolas' bare cock gently stretching his passage. As his lover slowly thrust into him, Jameson could see nothing but a look of pure love in Nicolas' kind blue eyes.

The whole experience seemed dreamlike. It felt quite surreal to be making tender love with his boyfriend in such a beautiful setting. The world was quiet except for the water lapping against their writhing bodies and the resulting cries of pleasure. It was almost as if they were the only ones in the world – well apart from all woodland creatures undoubtedly looking on with bemusement.

After some minutes, Nicolas stopped in his delectable toil long enough to slowly spin Jameson around onto his hands and knees, facing towards the campsite. The sensation as the cock rotated inside his passage caused Jameson eyes to roll back and a low moan of appreciation to escape his lips.

Once in position, Nicolas recommenced his carnal labors. The slow, steady pace from before was soon replaced with a more urgent pounding. The water splashed about the handsome couple, as Nicolas slammed away into Jameson's delicious derriere. After only a few minutes, Nicolas tightened his grip on Jameson's solid hips, as he grew ever closer to orgasm. Moments later, apparently unable to hold off any longer, he reached his climax and deposited his milky load deep inside his boyfriend's velvety passage.

Jameson felt the throbbing of the cock inside him and was happy to once again receive his boyfriend's cream...it was a feeling he was sure he'd never tire of. He was glad that they'd recently agreed to discard condoms and trust completely in one another. The throbbing gradually subsided and Nicolas' breathing returned to normal.

With his manhood still firmly wedged deep inside Jameson, Nicolas maneuvered them both back around again so that they were positioned half in the water with Jameson sitting in Nicolas' lap. Nicolas reached around and began to wank his boyfriend from behind. A handful of strokes later, Jameson seed shot upwards and splattered back down into the water. His body convulsed with every pleasurable spurt until finally his balls were spent.

Jameson lay back and rested his head against Nicolas' smooth, defined chest. They stayed there, both resting and enjoying the twilight as the sun set over mountains. As darkness fell, the air began to cool somewhat, but they were still comfortable enough in the water.

"I love you, Nico."

"I love you too, JJ."

* * *

The next day dawned clear and bright. When the pair emerged from the tent they thought the weather report must have been mistaken. After a hearty breakfast of fried eggs, baked beans and toast, they decided to explore their surroundings and go for a hike.

There were trails heading off in numerous directions but they decided to take the one that led to the closest summit. Jameson remembered climbing it just about every time he'd visited with his family and from memory the view from the top was spectacular. They set off, both sporting sturdy hiking boots, cargo shorts and singlets. In his knapsack Jameson had packed a picnic lunch and bottles of water.

It took more than an hour to reach to the top as the pair often stopped to admire their surroundings or found themselves in need of affection. It would be safe to say that their balls were considerably lighter by the time they cleared the last of the trees and were standing on the rocky peak.

The view was magnificent, the peak they were on was one of the highest in the mountain range, so they had an unobstructed view down towards Port Davinica and also westward over the mountains and down to the desert in the distance. Nicolas pulled his phone out of his pocket and snapped quite a few photos. They then took out their lunch and happily devoured the thick salad sandwiches, fruit and shortbread biscuits.

"Thanks so much for bringing me up here, JJ. I love it!" said Nicolas, giving his boyfriend a soft kiss on the lips.

"Well we can come back whenever you like." Jameson gave Nicolas' thigh a loving squeeze. "Although we'd have to rent a cabin in the wintertime, it gets might frosty."

"It'd be fantastic to play in the snow!" exclaimed Nicolas, with a childlike glee.

Just as they finished lunch, Jameson was looking out towards the north and could see dark clouds beginning to mass. There were still a long ways off, but given the ranger's warning the day before he thought it best that they play it safe.

"We should get headed back to camp. We don't want to be up here if a storm hits," said Jameson, pointing at the clouds.

"Sure," agreed Nicolas, obviously not relishing the thought of getting caught in the rain.

They quickly packed up and were headed back down the trail ten minutes later. They were about halfway down when they felt temperature start to drop rather rapidly. The gentle breeze from before had picked up quite considerably, causing the leaves to rustle loudly in the trees above them. The sunlight had also disappeared and the day became dark and dismal.

"I can't believe it's changed so quickly," said Nicolas, his voice carrying a note of concern.

"Yeah, the mountains can be like that. But hopefully we'll get back before it properly arrives."

Suddenly, there was a bright flash of lightning, followed five seconds later by a heavy crash of thunder. They could smell the approaching rain in the air.

"Dammit, it's closer than I thought," said Jameson. "We really need to get a move on, we're still about twenty minutes away."

The duo rushed as quickly as they could, taking care not to trip on any of the branches and rocks littering the path. About ten minutes later, they were both sweating from exertion, even with the much-reduced temperature. There had been several subsequent rounds of lightning and thunder, each time seeming just that little bit closer. It was then that the rain began to fall, lightly at first but soon building into a proper downpour. The trail soon became a mess of mud and both boys struggled to keep their footing. They were almost to the campsite when Nicolas tripped on a tree root and came crashing down, grazing his knees and banging his forearm.

"Nico!" Jameson cried out. "Are you OK?"

"Yeah, I think so," replied Nicolas, although his face was contracted in pain.

Jameson slowly helped him to his feet and Nicolas gingerly put weight on first his left foot and then the right.

"I'm just sore, nothing broken," Nicolas assured Jameson.

"Good! We're almost there," said Jameson, with forced cheerfulness.

By the time they reached the clearing they were both drenched. The rain seemed to be getting even heavier. Fortunately, they'd packed away their gear but the excess of water running along the ground was worrying. They quickly climbed into the tent and stripped out of their wet clothes and jumped into a sleeping bag together. Their body heat soon warmed them up.

"I hope we don't get swept away," said Jameson, trying to lighten the mood.

"It'll be just like a water bed," joked Nicolas, as he cuddled in close to his boyfriend.

Their hands ran over each other, gently caressing at first but their raging erections clearly showed their true intentions. Just then they heard the sound of a 4WD pulling up outside.

"Guys, are you there?" came Isaac's booming voice from outside.

"How does he manage to always come when we're naked," Nicolas whispered to Jameson.

"Yeah, we're here." Jameson called out in response.

He grabbed for a t-shirt to cover himself a little and unzipped the front of the tent.

"Sorry to disturb you again," said Isaac, apparently guessing what the boys had been in the process of doing. "I came by earlier but you weren't here. The weather service has upgraded the warning. This is just the beginning; it's going to get much worse."

As if to illustrate his point, there was an extremely bright lighting flash and a terrible clap of thunder. Jameson could practically feel the electricity rippling through the air.

"What do we do?" asked Jameson, glad that the ranger had come back for them.

"We've been told to evacuate all the campers to cabins. Unfortunately, they're all full now but you're welcome to the lounge room floor of mine."

"Sounds better than drowning or being electrocuted out here," said Jameson.

"I vote for life," added Nicolas, being cheeky.

"I'll help you pack up but we better hurry," said Isaac.

The boys quickly put on dry clothes and packed up their belongings. Thankfully, the tent was easy to dismantle, even in the pouring rain, and shortly they had everything bundled up in the ranger's car and were headed back to the cabin. Unfortunately, they had gotten waterlogged once more and both Jameson and Nicolas were starting to shiver.

"You can have a hot shower when we get back. Can't have my campers getting hypothermia," said Isaac, with a hearty laugh.

A few minutes later they were in the warm and safety of the Ranger's cabin. Isaac gave the boys two fluffy brown towels and showed them where the facilities were.

"Thanks so much for all your help," said Nicolas.

"It's my job," Isaac said humbly. "I don't mind if you two want to shower together but don't stay too long in there, as the hot water system isn't the best."

"We'll be quick, we promise," said Jameson.

The boys appreciated Isaac's open-minded attitude and promptly went to the bathroom to change out of their newly wet clothes and warm up again. They remained true to their word and resisted the temptation to take a long, leisurely shower, only staying under the pleasantly hot water, long enough to take the chill out of their bones.

Shortly afterwards they exited the bathroom in yet another fresh set of clothes – at this rate they'd have nothing left to wear home. Jameson noticed that while they'd showered Isaac has set up a roaring fire and there was also a delicious scent of chocolate wafting through the cabin.

Isaac appeared in the doorway of the kitchen with two steaming mugs.

"I've just made you some hot chocolate with a splash of brandy to ward off the cold," said Isaac, as he offered them the mugs.

"Can we take you home?" said Jameson, only half-joking.

Isaac broke into his loud laugh once more.

"My husband would probably object," Isaac responded, with a broad grin upon his face.

"Is he a ranger too?" asked Nicolas.

"No, he works overseas with Doctors without Borders, although he's scheduled to come back at the end of the month," answered Isaac.

"Wow. That must be tough; being separated," said Jameson.

"It is, but it makes the time we do get together all the more special. I'm just going to put your wet clothes in the dryer, why don't you sit down in front of the fire?" suggested Isaac.

They soon settled themselves on the plush dark brown sofa, as the heat enveloped them like a protective cocoon.

"I'm glad that you aren't off saving the world," said Jameson, snuggling into Nicolas.

"I could never leave you," Nicolas replied, pulling Jameson even closer to him.

Isaac soon returned and the trio chatted amiably for the next few hours while the storm continued to rage outside. The ranger proved to be delightful company and an even better cook...rustling up a delicious creamy chicken pasta for their dinner. They had just finished eating when all of a sudden, harsh white light filled the cabin and there was a deafening crack of thunder before they were plunged into darkness.

"Don't panic," said Isaac immediately. "Lightning probably just knocked out the generator. We'll still be safe inside here, don't you worry. Just stay where you are and I'll fetch some candles."

The soothing timbre of the ranger's voice had a reassuring effect on both the boys. They stayed at the table while Isaac rectified the situation and soon the cabin was bathed in the soft, soothing glow of candlelight. After the day's adventures both Jameson and Nicolas were having trouble stifling their yawns.

"I think it's time for bed. I dare say I'll have a lot of clearing up to do tomorrow," said Isaac.

The ranger then disappeared briefly but soon reentered the lounge room with a supply of blankets and pillows to prepare a makeshift bed for the weary lads. In practically no time, there was a cozy spot set up alongside the fire.

"See you in the morning," said Isaac.

"Goodnight," the boys replied in unison.

Jameson and Nicolas climbed under the covers and cuddled up together.

"This is still kinda romantic," whispered Nicolas.

"It is. Sweet dreams, barista boy."

The pair soon drifted off with the sound of the fire crackling beside them and the rain beating down on the wooden roof of the cabin.

The next morning they awoke to sun streaming through the windows and the appetizing smell of bacon. The ranger was apparently already up and making breakfast.

"This guy is amazing," said Nicolas sleepily.

"Don't you go getting any ideas Mister, you're all mine," stated Jameson, squeezing Nicolas tight.

"Morning guys, food will be ready in ten if you want to have a quick shower?" Isaac said from the doorway.

"Thanks, we will," said Jameson.

They quickly made themselves presentable and keenly wolfed down the hearty breakfast the ranger had prepared for them. In an effort to repay all of his kindness, they offered to help Isaac with his work. The trio spent a good part of the day clearing branches from the roads and rescuing the occasional trapped furry creature. When they were done Isaac drove them back to their campsite and helped them re-setup. The ranger bade them farewell and left them to spend their final night in the mountains alone.

Later that evening, as he and Nicolas lay side-by-side, holding hands, on a blanket looking up the star soaked sky, Jameson couldn't remember being happier. It wasn't quite the weekend he'd imagined but it had been enjoyable nonetheless.

If only we could stay here forever.

* * *

Both the boys were in a rather good mood after their time away, but were looking forward to being back in the city. Thankfully, the traffic back to Port Davinica wasn't too heavy and they made it back in just less than three hours.

They parked right in front of Jameson's townhouse, the leafy trees providing a nice shady spot to protect against the summer heat. Jameson quickly hopped out and went to unlock the front door – his bladder had reached capacity about half an hour beforehand – while Nicolas started to unload the camping equipment and their bags. He raced through the door and straight through to the bathroom on the ground floor.

It wasn't until after he relieved himself and was on his way back outside to help Nicolas with the bags that he realized that something was wrong. One of the French doors leading out to the terrace was standing wide open with its glass broken and scattered on the floor.

"Nico!" yelled Jameson. "Nico! I need you!"

"What? What's wrong?" said Nicolas, as he ran in through the open front door.

"Someone's broken in!" exclaimed Jameson.

"Are they still here?" asked Nicolas, in a hushed whisper.

"I don't know," said Jameson, becoming increasingly distraught.

"Come outside, we'll call the police from there," suggested Nicolas.

"OK."

Ten minutes later a police car arrived and Jameson was relieved to see it was the two officers he'd met after the incident in the car park.

"Mr James, sorry to see you again in such unpleasant circumstances," said Officer Ford. "Are the intruders still on the premises?"

"I don't know, we only just got home and came straight back out when we saw the broken back door, but we haven't seen or heard anything else," said Jameson.

"You two stay here, Officer Rayles and myself will have a walk through just to be sure," instructed Officer Ford.

For Jameson, it felt like an eternity had passed before the officers reappeared, although when he checked his watch he saw that only a few minutes had gone by.

"OK, there's no one in there but you should prepare yourself. It's a bit nasty in there. You can have a look around but it's best not to touch anything until our forensics team has been by. I've already put a call into them," said Officer Ford.

Jameson and Nicolas accompanied the officers back inside to inspect the damage. The kitchen was a mess with all the food pulled out of the fridge and the cupboards, and smeared all over the place. By the look of the way it was congealed on the floor, the break-in had happened at least the previous day. Every room they went into had been touched in some way, some worse than others. There was chaos everywhere they turned…drawers had been rifled through, wardrobes emptied, little knickknacks destroyed. Strangely, nothing of value seemed to be missing.

The most disturbing part was that not only had every single mirror in the townhouse been smashed, but also had had the word 'WHORE' scrawled in bright red across them. Jameson felt nauseous. At first he'd thought it was written in blood but upon closer inspection it proved to be paint. Jameson was close to tears but didn't want to turn into a blubbering mess in front of the officers.

"It will be OK," said Nicolas, as he gave Jameson a quick reassuring hug.

By this time the forensics team had arrived, so Officer Ford took Jameson and Nicolas into the backyard to talk while his colleagues completed their work.

"Now Mr James…can I call you Jameson?" asked Officer Ford, apparently deciding to take a softer approach.

"Yes, that's fine and this is my boyfriend Nicolas."

"Good to meet you. You, can call me Brad," said Officer Ford. "Now, I know this is a difficult time and I'll try not to keep you too long. It looks to us like this was a more personal attack rather than just a random break-in. The lack of theft and the vandalism suggests someone carrying a grudge. Does anyone come to mind?"

"No, no one!" said Jameson, appalled at the idea that someone he knew could have done this.

"Me neither. Everyone likes Jameson," added Nicolas. "Although there were those gifts left on the doorstep."

"What gifts were these?" asked Brad.

"Just some roses and a box of chocolates. We just thought it was a harmless fan," said Jameson.

"A fan?" Brad's interest was clearly piqued.

"Oh, I'm a writer. I'm no J K Rowling but I've gotten a few letters. None of them were threatening though," explained Jameson, still trying to fathom who could have done this.

"I'd like to take a look at those if you don't mind," said Brad.

"No, of course not. They are up in my study, I'll get them when your people have finished," offered Jameson, eager to help.

"What about all the missing stuff?" asked Nicolas.

"The poltergeist? Nah, that was probably nothing," Jameson said dismissively.

"In cases like this it's best to explore every option," countered Brad.

"Well it was just a bunch of things, nothing valuable, that disappeared and then reappeared later. We didn't think much of it," said Jameson.

The reality of what may have been happening began to slowly dawn on him.

That will teach me to joke about stalkers.

"I honestly don't know who would do this," said Jameson, a touch of despair creeping into his voice.

"Have you had any relationships end badly?" asked Brad, emanating concern.

"Well the last one was a disaster, but he dumped me. If anyone had reason for vengeance it was me."

"We should talk to him, just to be thorough," said Brad.

"OK, I'll give you his details. Although I haven't talked to him in over six months."

There was more than just a tinge of bitterness in Jameson's voice.

"Thank you. Believe me, I know how difficult this is. I've been the victim of stalking myself. It can leave you feeling powerless and angry, but I promise you, we will do everything we can to help put a stop to it," said Brad firmly.

"Did they catch yours?" asked Jameson.

"It took a while, but yes they did."

A cloud seemed to cross his face at the evidently unpleasant memory.

"How can we keep him safe?" asked Nicolas, understandably concerned for his boyfriend's wellbeing.

"Take simple precautions. I'd recommend you carry a deterrent, like pepper spray, with you at all times and avoid situations where you're alone in badly lit areas. Predators like this look for opportunities when you'll be vulnerable. Here is my card and I want you to feel free to call me at any time if you have any questions or if you feel like you're in danger." Brad handed cards to both the boys. "The same goes for you Nicolas. You may become a target as well, if the stalker can't access Jameson. I don't want to frighten you too much but you do need to take the situation very seriously."

"Don't worry, we are," said Nicolas, his protective side clearly showing.

"Thank you so much, Brad; I really appreciate all your help," said Jameson.

"No problem. Like I said, I've been where you are and I want to make sure you stay safe. I'll just check and see how the guys are going inside and I'll be back shortly."

When he'd gone Nicolas gave Jameson a very strong, reassuring hug.

"We're sleeping at my place tonight and we are buying you protection tomorrow," said Nicolas with authority.

"But we don't use condoms anymore," joked Jameson.

"Ha, ha…so funny. Now be serious, I don't know what I'd do if anything ever happened to you."

Nicolas gave Jameson another strong hug.

"You can't get rid of me that easily," said Jameson, still trying to keep the conservation light-hearted.

Despite his best efforts, however, there was a feeling of dread building in his stomach.

Who could have done this?

Brad returned shortly afterwards and told them that the forensic team was packing up and that they would soon have the place to themselves. Around ten minutes, later they were alone once more and they had just begun to tidy the kitchen when Matt and Trent rushed in.

"We saw the police cars leaving! Are you guys OK?" demanded Matt, the worry evident in his voice.

"Break-in?" asked Trent, after apparently noticing the mess on the floor.

So Jameson recounted the story for them and saw the growing horror on their faces when he got to the part about the mirrors and revelation that he had a stalker.

"I wish we could help but we were out partying most of the weekend so didn't notice a thing," lamented Matt, with a sad expression.

"It's fine, I'm sure the police can handle it, but we do need some help tidying up the house if you're keen?" suggested Jameson hopefully.

The task had seemed far too daunting for just Nicolas and himself.

"Of course," said Matt.

"Sure thing," agreed Trent.

With the four of them working together they had the townhouse relatively tidy after a few hours, although there was still the matter of the broken back door and mirrors. In the end they decided to simply throw away the shards of glass and look into replacing the actual mirrors later, while they nailed a piece of wood to the door to temporarily fix the problem.

As night fell, Matt and Trent retreated back to their apartment and Jameson packed a bag to go stay at Nicolas' place. Jameson left the house feeling violated and more than a bit frightened. He was still unable to believe that someone was targeting him like this.

It wasn't until after they'd showered and had climbed into Nicolas' comfy queen-sized bed together that Jameson started to feel somewhat less vulnerable. He clung to Nicolas, not out of sexual need, but for the sense of strength and security. Despite the harrowing events of the day, they soon drifted off, although for Jameson his sleep was anything but restful with his dreams plagued with shadowy figures lying in wait.

* * *

Three weeks passed and neither the police nor Ruby had turned up any leads. The forensics team hadn't turned up any unexpected fingerprints or DNA. Jameson was a tad disappointed as he'd been hoping for a CSI-like resolution where the culprit was caught by a microscopic trace of African bee pollen he'd left behind.

Damn television and its unrealistic depiction of police work.

Ruby, who'd been equal parts appalled and angry upon hearing the news, had even set up cameras outside the townhouse, in the hopes of catching someone loitering suspiciously, all to no avail.

Since there'd been no more mysterious gifts or items disappearing from the house Jameson had begun to relax a bit. Not to say that he wasn't being careful. Ruby had bought him a small taser for protection, which he carried with him most of the time, but he didn't want to live the rest of his life in fear. Jameson had already locked himself away in the house twice before and he had no intention of doing it again.

Besides, there might be nothing to worry about any more...probably.

It was around this time that Jameson decided to put his past well and truly behind him. Over the last few months both David and Judd had tried to contact Jameson but he had rebuffed all attempts, ignoring their calls and texts. Jameson knew that if he wanted to move forward he needed to properly deal with the carnage the pair had inflicted on his emotional self by facing them. Dr. Waters had been gently encouraging him to do just that for quite some time. Jameson had been putting off the unpleasant chore, as he wasn't sure whether or not he'd ever be ready to see them without fear of a double homicide.

What had finally changed his mind was Nicolas. He'd woken up the previous Sunday morning and seen his beautiful boyfriend sleeping peacefully beside him and was filled with such an overwhelming sense of love it nearly took his breath away. Jameson realized that he was happier than he'd ever been with David and that it was time to forgive the duplicitous duo.

So, a few days later there they sat, in a painfully awkward silence, as they waited for their drinks to arrive. Jameson had arranged to meet them on neutral ground in a chain café in midtown. It was noisy, filled with families, and not somewhere one wanted to spend a lot of time. Once they had their drinks in hand, Jameson began the conversation he'd practiced in his head so many times since that fateful day when they'd crushed his heart.

"Thank you for coming," said Jameson, in a calm voice.

"Thanks for reaching out to us," replied David.

"I thought it was time," continued Jameson.

"You look really good," remarked Judd.

"Thank you."

He felt no need to return the compliment, despite both of them looking as good as he'd remembered.

"I just want to say how sorry we both are for…" began David.

"Stop," said Jameson, cutting him off mid-sentence. "I don't need to hear it. As badly as you two acted, I don't hate you. Don't get me wrong, I did. I wanted the both of you to die slow painful deaths."

David and Judd stared at Jameson, both with concerned looks upon their faces.

"But, I've moved on. I'm really happy now," said Jameson truthfully.

"I'm glad to hear it," said David, obviously relieved.

"Me too," added Judd. "I was afraid you'd never talk to us again…I miss my best friend."

"That's unfortunate, and I missed you too, but don't misunderstand; I forgive you but I can't forget. So, while I don't hold any malice towards you I will never be able to trust either one of you ever again," said Jameson, his voice remaining neutral.

It was very different from the violent screaming match he had envisioned in his darker moments. Jameson noted the looks of disappointment on their faces but he wasn't moved; in fact, he felt nothing towards them at all.

"I wish you both the best but I don't think we belong in each other's lives anymore," said Jameson evenly.

Neither of the pair offered any response. Jameson finished his coffee and put some money on the table.

"Have a nice weekend."

Jameson got up and exited the café, without a backward glance. He felt lighter than he had in a long time. It was if an invisible weight he hadn't known he was still carrying had finally been lifted. A broad smile filled Jameson's face and he went back home to where Nicolas was waiting for him with open arms...and hopefully legs.

9

Nicolas was headed back to Montréal for the weekend, with his sister, to see their father. He was doing much better but after the scare both siblings had an understandable need to spend more time together with him.

"Enjoy yourself while I'm away...but not too much," said Nicolas giving his boyfriend's alluring, plump ass a playful slap.

"Miss you already."

Jameson leaned into give Nicolas a long lingering goodbye kiss. Not wanting to sit at home like a lovelorn puppy, Jameson organized to meet up with Connor and Didier at a new gay bar that had opened up just around the corner from Graywood Gardens – there was a readymade clientele, after all.

The aviation themed bar – Cockpit – was quite packed, the two-for-one cocktail special no doubt helping. Jameson would have had invited Matt and Trent to come along as well, but they were away for the weekend for the wedding of Trent's sister.

When Jameson arrived he was surprised to see an unhappy looking Jacob chatting with Connor and Didier at the bar.

"Hi guys, everything OK?" asked Jameson, selfishly hoping whatever the problem was it wasn't going to spoil their night.

"Andy cheated on me," said Jacob.

"Oh I'm sorry to hear that. Believe me I know how you feel," commiserated Jameson.

In an attempt to cheer Jacob up they proceeded to have quite a few cocktails and mercilessly discussed Andy's failings – both real and imagined.

A few hours later Jacob seemed to be much better spirits and Jameson was glad to have been able to help a fellow scorned soul. It was getting late and the lads decided to call it a night.

"We're going to get a cab, do you want us to drop you on the way?" offered Connor.

"Nah, I need to sober up a bit and it's not far to walk," answered Jameson.

"Do you mind if I join you for some of the way, I think I need a bit of fresh air too," said Jacob, his words slightly slurred and looking a little unsteady on his feet.

"Sure no problem."

After the cab had gone Jameson and Jacob went off on their merry way. They turned into the small alley that ran alongside Graywood Gardens, which was deserted apart from them and reeked of stale urine.

Ergh why can't they use a toilet!

Their footsteps echoed against the side of building as they walked. They were halfway along the alley when Jacob suddenly turned to Jameson and kissed him. Surprised, and more than a little drunk, it took Jameson a few moments to register what was happening and to push Jacob away.

"Someone's had too many cocktails," said Jameson, trying to make light of the situation. He figured it was just a drunken lapse of judgment on Jacob's behalf.

"Why aren't I good enough?" asked Jacob sharply.

"What?"

"How is that little slut better than me?" continued Jacob, his voice full of anger.

"You mean Nicolas? I know you're upset about Andy but you can't talk about my boyfriend like that."

"I don't give a fuck about Andy! Why can't you see that we belong together?"

Jameson began to sober up at a rapid place, as it finally dawned on him what was going on.

"It was you?" asked Jameson incredulously.

"You never even gave us a chance! I could make you so happy!"

"I'm sorry if I gave you the wrong idea but there was never any us."

Despite his initial instinct to try and defuse the situation, Jameson felt himself getting angry.

"You wrecked my house! You're sick!" said Jameson, his voice rising.

"I will make you love me," yelled Jacob as he rushed forward, knocking Jameson to the ground.

Jameson was stunned at first; he didn't know what to do. He'd never gotten around to taking those self-defense classes.

Why didn't I bring my taser?

They wrestled on the filthy ground, their clothes ripping and becoming increasingly covered in grime. Jameson looked up and saw Jacob's face contorted with rage; he didn't recognize the person behind those wild eyes. Jacob kept attempting to kiss him, over and over, while Jameson moved his head away in disgust.

As Jameson struggled against Jacob's vice-like grip, his body began to ache with the exertion. He realized that he'd have to try and fight his way out. Jameson felt a sudden surge of adrenaline, as his primal survival instincts kicked in. Calling upon all his strength, Jameson ripped his right arm free and managed to punch Jacob squarely in the nose. It was enough to startle and distract his attacker long enough for Jameson to gain the advantage. He pushed upwards, knocking Jacob to the side and struggled to his feet.

I've got to get away!

Unfortunately, Jameson only got a few paces before he was tackled to the ground. His head smacked hard into the ground making his vision swim. Jameson felt his t-shirt rip completely open as Jacob pinned him to the cement.

Lying helpless on the grubby ground Jameson suddenly felt Jacob's erection digging into him.

Surely he can't be enjoying this?!?

Just then Jacob yanked at Jameson's jeans, popping the button fly and managing to pull them halfway down over Jameson's buttocks. After a sickening realization about what Jacob meant to do, Jameson began to struggle furiously.

"No, please," begged Jameson.

"Stop pretending you don't like it!" screamed Jacob.

Jameson knew he had to try and do something to stop the assault. He jerked his head back and felt a searing bolt of pain when it connected with Jacob's face. Jameson felt Jacob's weight lift off of him and he frantically tried to crawl forward. Sadly, the blow to the head hadn't been enough to stop his attacker and Jameson soon felt Jacob's hands grabbing for him.

Jacob spun Jameson onto his back and punched him in the face before straddling him once more.

"You fucking bastard. I'm going to make you pay. You don't deserve my love!" spat Jacob.

"Please, Jacob. Don't do…" pleaded Jameson, starting to beg again.

He was cut off mid-plea when Jacob slid his hands up around Jameson's neck and began to squeeze. Jameson struggled to breathe and began to feel dizzy.

"Hey what's going on?" called a distant voice.

Jameson felt the pressure on his neck lesson and was able to call out "Help!" with a raspy voice. There was a rushing of footsteps as shadowy figures raced into the alley. Jameson felt Jacob jump off of him and take off running.

Gasping for breath Jameson tried to sit up but immediately collapsed back down again. His saviors soon reached him and were doing their best to comfort him. Jameson wasn't sure how many people had come to his rescue, he was still feeling light-headed and only heard a jumble of voices.

"Don't try to move. It'll be OK," said one of the good Samaritans.

"Someone call the police…"

"Oh my God, he's bleeding, I think he needs an ambulance…"

Jameson wondered who they were talking about. He could feel wetness running down his face but had thought it was just sweat. It wasn't until he put his hand up to check that Jameson saw the blood and realized he was more injured than he'd thought.

Only a few minutes passed before the sounds of approaching sirens filled the night air. The paramedics were the first to arrive, parking at the top of the alley, as it was too narrow for the ambulance to pass. They quickly made their way on foot to Jameson's side.

"Can you tell me your name?" asked the blond paramedic.

"Jameson."

"Where does it hurt?"

"Everywhere!"

Jameson had started to feel his injuries now that the adrenaline was wearing off. After a cursory examination the paramedics moved him so they could treat him in the brighter light of the ambulance. There were various scrapes on his arms and a nasty gash on his forehead that they efficiently cleaned and bandaged.

"Follow my finger with your eyes," instructed the other paramedic.

Jameson did the best he could, although he was feeling a little woozy. Apparently, the paramedic was satisfied with the result.

"Now, we are going to take you to the hospital to take some x-rays and make sure that you're OK, but first the police would like to ask you a few questions. Do you feel up to that?" asked the blond paramedic.

"I think so…sure." Jameson was a little dazed and no doubt suffering from shock but he wanted to help them catch his attacker.

"Hello, Jameson, isn't it?" asked a big bear of a policeman.

Jameson nodded.

"I'm Officer Danvers. Can you tell us what happened tonight?" asked the officer.

"Jacob attacked me," said Jameson, still struggling to believe that it was real.

"Is this Jacob a friend of yours?" asked Officer Danvers.

"Yes…No…I mean…" Jameson was starting to become confused.

"That's OK buddy. Take your time," said Officer Danvers patiently.

"He's more friends with friends of mine. I think he's been stalking me. Brad…I mean Officer Brad Ford knows about it…the stalking that is."

Jameson was worried he wasn't making much sense and wished that Brad was here now so that he didn't have to try and explain everything all over again.

"Alright we'll contact him. Do you know Jacob's last name?" asked Officer Danvers.

"Fields…I think. I'm not sure," said Jameson, not feeling particularly helpful.

"OK, that's enough for now, we'll talk to you again after you've been treated at the hospital. Can we contact anyone for you?" asked Officer Danvers, in a sympathetic tone.

"No, I can call…" Jameson went to retrieve his phone from the pocket of his jeans, only to discovered that his phone had been smashed in the attack. "Actually, yes if you could call a few people that would be great," said Jameson, giving the officer Connor and Ruby's numbers from memory.

He wanted to call Nicolas himself from the hospital. *Don't want to frighten him more than I have to.*

Jameson was remarkably composed given what had happened but he was beginning to feel tired and was grateful that the police interview was over for now. The blond paramedic helped him back into the ambulance and Jameson lay down on the stretcher. The next few hours passed in a blur of tests, with various doctors and nurses checking in on him. He was placed in a private room but the smell of antiseptic still hung heavy in the air and the distant cries of people in the ER filtered through the corridors.

Ruby arrived first with Connor and Didier only a few minutes behind.

"Oh my god! I will kill him!" stated Ruby with fury in her eyes, after seeing Jameson's swollen nose, blackened eye and stitched forehead.

"I'm so sorry. I had no idea," said Connor, his face awash with guilt, obviously blaming himself for introducing them.

"We've told the police everything we know about Jacob. Is there anything else we can do?" asked Didier, clearly sharing the guilt.

With the protective circle of his friends there Jameson's veneer of calm started to fall away and he began to sob. Connor held him as the pent-up emotion of the night was released. A few minutes later, the tears stopped flowing and Jameson began to feel far less fragile.

By this time, it was around 4am and Jameson realized he still hadn't called his boyfriend. He was reluctant to worry him, seeing he was so far away, but knew he'd want to know if the situation was reversed.

"Can I borrow your phone? Mine was broken. I need to ring Nicolas," Jameson asked Connor.

"Of course, will he be awake?"

"Yeah, with the time difference he should be having breakfast," said Jameson, after quickly doing the math.

"Do you want some privacy?" asked Ruby gently.

"No it's fine, you guys can stay. Besides, I don't really feel like being alone," said Jameson, his voice wavering slightly.

And so, with his trio of friends watching, he made the difficult call.

"Hi Nico, it's me…yeah it is really late here. Now, don't freak out but I thought you should know that I'm in the hospital…I was attacked…no, I'm OK…no, nothing broken, I'm just a bit bruised and battered…the guys are here with me and they're looking after me…yes, I do know who…it was Jacob…no, I don't know where he is, the police are looking for him…Ruby said the same, but I don't think murder is the best option…are you sure?...what about your dad?...OK, I'll see you this afternoon…I love you too."

Just as he finished his call a stressed-looking, young doctor came back in.

"Mr James your x-rays have come back clear and there are no signs of concussion but you shouldn't drive for the next few days. We are happy to release you but you'll need to come back and get your stitches removed in about a week. Are you alright to get home?"

"Yes I am. Thank you very much Doctor."

Connor and Ruby helped him to Didier's car and the foursome drove directly to Jameson's townhouse. Once there, his three friends insisted on staying the rest of the night, not wanting to leave him alone, especially with Jacob's whereabouts unknown. Jameson was grateful for the company and he certainly had the room.

Connor accompanied Jameson upstairs to his bedroom and helped him change into something to sleep in. Only when Jameson was safely tucked up in bed did Connor seem comfortable leaving.

"Now, just yell out if you need anything," commanded Connor.

"Yes, Sir," answered Jameson solemnly.

"Good boy, sleep well."

Connor switched off the light and gently closed the door behind him.

The painkillers that the doctor prescribed soon took effect and Jameson fell into in a deep, dreamless sleep.

* * *

Around eleven, Connor, Didier and Ruby were in the kitchen making breakfast when there was a firm knock on the front door.

"I'll get it, you keep an eye on the pancakes," Ruby instructed Connor. "And you can finish the coffees," she said to Didier.

"Yes Ma am," they replied in unison, exchanging a cheeky look.

"I prefer Mistress," said Ruby, as she exited the kitchen with a sassy strut.

She opened to the door to the sight of a strapping policeman in uniform.

"Well, hello there, Officer Ford!" said Ruby, almost purring her words.

"Good morning, Miss Washington. I was hoping to speak with Jameson."

"Please call me Ruby. He's upstairs resting in bed, we were just about to have breakfast if you'd like to join us." Ruby was using the full force of her charm.

"Ruby, leave the poor man alone," called Jameson, from the base of the stairs.

The mouthwatering cooking smells had woken him up and dragged him from his bed. "Although you're certainly welcome to join us Brad," added Jameson.

"You should've stayed in bed, we would have brought breakfast up to you," admonished Ruby.

"Jameson, how are you feeling?" Brad asked.

"Sore, but better than before. Brad, this is Connor and Didier," said Jameson, indicating his friends who had just exited the kitchen carrying plates of food. "Why don't we go out and sit on the terrace? We can talk and eat out there."

"Only if you're feeling up to it," said Brad.

"Yeah the fresh air will do me good." Jameson was trying to be cheerful, in spite of the situation.

After they were settled, Brad filled the group in on what had occurred overnight.

"We tracked down Jacob in his apartment. He had taken a bottleful of pills and was unconscious but fortunately they were able to get him to the hospital in time and pump his stomach."

"Oh my God, is he OK?" asked Didier. "I'm sorry Jameson, I didn't mean…"

"No, it's fine. He's your friend too, I know that you're concerned," said Jameson with a calmness and understanding that surprised even himself, given what he'd been through.

"Yes, he's in a stable condition."

"What will happen now?" asked Jameson. "Will he be charged?"

"Yes, most likely, but it will all depend on the psychiatric assessment as to how we proceed. Right now he's being held in custody. He seems to be a very disturbed young man," answered Brad. "But I can assure you that you're no longer in danger from him."

"Thank goodness for that," gushed Ruby, her relief evident.

"Thank you, for letting me know," said Jameson. "And thanks for breakfast guys, it looks delicious."

There was a somber mood around the table, despite the relatively good news of Jacob no longer being at large.

"Come up, cheer up. I'm going to be fine and Jacob will get the help he needs. I'm the invalid here and I refuse to wallow so neither should any of you. Now, smile before I really get stroppy!" threatened Jameson, in a light-hearted manner.

He had had enough misery to last him for quite a while and now all he wanted to do is keep moving forward and appreciate what he had.

"The boy's right. Who wants mimosas?" asked Ruby.

"Yes please!" was the resounding chorus from the table, excepting Brad.

"I'm still on duty so I'm afraid I must decline, but I'm glad to see you in such good spirits Jameson. I should get going but you have my number if you need anything."

"Thank you, I really appreciate it," said Jameson, grateful to have the muscular policeman looking out for him.

"I'll see myself out. Enjoy the rest of your weekend."

Brad left the terrace and exited through the side garden gate.

"Wonder if he'd mind if I called to get my needs met?" Ruby asked playfully.

"You're incorrigible," said Connor. "Although, I don't think he'd be too opposed."

"Well you're welcome to him, I'm happy with my current boy thank you very much," remarked Jameson.

As if by magic, Nicolas appeared on the terrace, wheeling his travel bag in behind him. He immediately rushed to give his injured boyfriend a huge hug, which caused Jameson to wince in pain as his bruised ribs cried out in protest.

"Owww…easy does it," said Jameson, trying not to show how much he was hurting.

"I'm so sorry. Are you OK? What can I do?"

Nicolas was desperate to help and obviously trying to compensate for not being there during the attack.

"I'm fine, I'm just glad you're back." Jameson reassured Nicolas by giving him a long, loving kiss.

"Don't mind us boys," joked Connor.

"Personally, I'm rather enjoying the show," added Ruby, with an infectious laugh.

Jameson broke his kiss briefly to sick his tongue out at his friends and put his lips right back onto Nicolas'. Eventually, they resurfaced for air.

"Better than any painkillers," said Jameson, with a contented smile. "Hungry?"

"No, I ate on the plane but I'd love a drink!" said Nicolas.

"Mimosas!" proclaimed Ruby, retreating to the kitchen, dragging Connor with her.

Didier moved around to the other side of table so that Nicolas could sit next to Jameson.

Despite his injuries, Jameson felt extremely lucky to be surrounded by his paramour and friends. He took Nicolas' hand in his and smiled.

Life isn't so bad.

* * *

Over the following month, Jameson took things easy while he was recovering, although after a few weeks he was back to light exercise at the gym.

Despite his rather calm attitude at the time, he had since had bouts of anger and blaming himself for the attack, which in turn had caused a few sleepless nights. He felt anxious about leaving the townhouse and didn't like to go anywhere alone.

Jameson began to see Dr. Waters twice a week to help him process what had happened. The good doctor had been horrified by the attack when she'd heard the news.

"I had no idea he was capable of anything like this," said Dr Waters mournfully.

Not that Jameson blamed her, as he realized Jacob was obviously very troubled and clearly needed more help than Dr Waters could provide. Initially, Jameson eagerly accepted her offer of a prescription to help with his issues but stopped taking the anxiety medication a few weeks later.

"Are you sure you should?" asked Nicolas, his eyes full of concern.

"I need to work through this without the pills," Jameson had explained.

Jameson used relaxation exercises that Dr Waters had taught him and he felt his fears lessoning as the weeks progressed. There was still one thing, however, that Jameson hadn't had the courage to do – to face Jacob again.

Jacob had pleaded guilty to the stalking and the attack, so there had been no need for Jameson to testify, which had left him missing a sense of closure. Jacob was currently in the criminal wing of Rosehaven Hospital where he was likely to remain for some time.

Encouraged by Dr Waters, and after first checking with Jacob's doctor, Jameson went to visit his former stalker.

"I'm going with you," Nicolas had insisted.

"Yes, but I think I should see him alone."

Nicolas begrudgingly agreed.

"I'll be right here if you need me," said Nicolas, when they were in the waiting room outside Jacob's ward.

"I know and I love you for it."

Jameson gave Nicolas a loving peck on the lips, took a deep breath and walked down the hall to the visiting room. He was reassured to see two security guards in the room when he entered, not that he expected there to be any trouble but his last encounter with Jacob hadn't been the most friendly. There was a sterile feel to the air and Jameson thought he could hear the occasional muffled yelling in the distance…possibly just his overactive imagination but you never can tell.

Jacob was already seated at a small table, wearing the standard uniform for the inmates – a loose white t-shirt and drab green pants. He looked up as Jameson approached with a mixture of fear and sorrow in his eyes. Any remaining trepidation that Jameson had been feeling melted away at the pitiful sight. To help break the tension Jameson sat down and gave Jacob a tightlipped smile.

"Jameson, I'm so, so sorry. I didn't mean to hurt you but I…" began Jacob meekly.

"Please, stop," said Jameson, cutting Jacob off mid-sentence. "I appreciate that you want to explain but I need to speak first, OK?"

Jacob nodded, the look of fear still present in his eyes.

"I don't hate you and I'm not angry with you…not any more. I know that it wasn't all your fault. You have problems and I'm glad that you're getting help."

Across the table Jacob started to relax a little.

"The medication and therapy is really helping but I think it will be a long while before I'm back to 'normal'."

"I'm glad to hear it. I want you to know that I forgive you for what you did," said Jameson, feeling lighter.

"Thank you so much! That means the world to me."

Tears began to form in the corner of Jacob's eyes.

"That being said, I think it would be better if we didn't see each other again," continued Jameson softly.

"I…I understand," said Jacob, the disappointment clear in his face.

"I have to go now but I do wish you the best for your recovery," said Jameson, trying to politely end the conversation.

"Thank you for coming. I never expected…thank you."

"Goodbye, Jacob."

Jameson got up and calmly walked to the door, he turned before he exited and gave Jacob a small smile of encouragement. He closed the door behind him and walked back down the corridor to his waiting boyfriend.

"Did everything go OK?" asked Nicolas, nervously jumping to his feet as soon as he spotted Jameson.

"Yeah, I just need a really big hug," answered Jameson.

"As you wish, my love."

Nicolas wrapped his arms around his noticeably emotional boyfriend. Jameson could have happily stayed in the embrace for hours but he needed to be outside away from the hospital atmosphere.

"Time to go," commanded Jameson. The handsome couple walked hand in hand, out of the hospital, and into the sunshine.

* * *

Jameson could hardly believe he was there, dressed in a dashing, charcoal gray suit with this beloved by his side. They, along with about fifty well-wishers, were standing in a white marquee, on a bluff overlooking the ocean. The sky was bright and clear, a light breeze keeping the day from becoming too hot. All in all, a perfect day for a wedding.

Not Nicolas and Jameson's, mind you…not just yet, at any rate. Rather they were attending the nuptials of Nicolas' friends, Adam and Steve.

The grooms were resplendent in matching navy blue suits with white shirts and black ties. The ceremony was beautiful with nary a dry eye in the house as the boys pledged their undying love and devotion to one another. Currently, the assembled crowd was seated for the reception and enjoying a scrumptious chicken and eggplant risotto for their entree.

It was the first wedding he'd gone to since his aborted one and Jameson was surprised at how well he was taking it all. Naturally, Jameson had been nervous in the days leading up to it, worried that it would bring back all sorts of painful memories. Indeed, he'd nearly said 'no' when Nicolas had first invited him to come along but had eventually seen sense.

I can't avoid weddings for the rest of my life, besides it's selfish to make it all about me.

He's discussed his fears with Connor the week beforehand not wanting to burden Nicolas with his niggling doubts – not when everything was finally going so well with them. After his third glass of champagne Jameson realized that he hadn't thought about David even once during the ceremony. In fact, all he had been thinking about was how much he loved Nicolas and how lucky he was to have found true love.

It turned out that Jameson recognized a great many of the guests, for a medium sized city, Port Davinica could seem rather small at times. Funnily enough, Connor and Didier were also in attendance – Connor and Adam having been friends since high school.

"How you holding up?" Connor had discreetly asked after the desserts had been served.

"I'm actually having a great time," Jameson said honestly. "But you're sweet for worrying."

The hours flew by and before too long the tables had been moved to the side and the dancing had begun in earnest.

Jameson noticed various guests pairing off and wandering away from time to time, only to reappear looking slightly disheveled with happy expressions – well one expected that sort of thing at any wedding really.

Jameson and Nicolas danced until the wee hours, with many a slow dance, and were one of the last couples left on the floor. It was a time of new beginnings and in keeping with that spirit Jameson decided to take a major leap of faith and take the next step in his relationship with Nicolas. High above them millions of stars twinkled down and Jameson couldn't think of a more romantic setting.

"There's something I've been wanting to ask you for a little while now," said Jameson, softly into Nicolas' ear.

"I'm listening."

Jameson broke apart from their dance hold and looked Nicolas directly in the eyes. He couldn't believe this beautiful man belonged to him.

"You know how much you mean to me. I couldn't imagine my life without you. I love you, Nico," said Jameson, his voice wavering with emotion.

"I love you too. Now what's your question," demanded Nicolas, with an air of mock impatience.

"Nicolas Nightingale, will you do me the honor of…moving in with me?" asked Jameson cautiously.

"Yes, of course I will. I thought you'd never ask!"

Feeling overjoyed, Jameson moved forward to give his paramour a slow passionate kiss.

* * *

To commemorate the occasion of Nicolas moving in, the new live-in lovers decided to host a grand housewarming. To add a touch of fun to the soirée, they decided to have a themed party – Alice in Wonderland. It was Nicolas' favorite book from his childhood and one Jameson had also been rather partial to.

Jameson was resplendent in a mismatched suit, a cacophony of colored ties and a peacock feather placed at a jaunty angle in his marvelous Mad Hatter Top Hat. Nicolas had decided upon a less is more approach as The White Rabbit, with small spectacles perched on his nose, bunny ears atop his head and a pair of tiny white shorts with a cute little cottontail attached at the back. Jameson felt a strong compulsion to squeeze said tail whilst they were getting ready and throughout the party as well – although he was hardly alone in that desire. Nicolas' sister, Nora, had arrived early to help them set up for the party. When they were ready she'd donned a blonde wig, blue dress and was transformed into their very own Alice.

Matt and Trent arrived first, unsurprising seeing they literally lived downstairs. The pair looked adorable in the matching outfits of Tweedledee and Tweedledum, although the shorts they were sporting didn't leave a great deal to the imagination...not that Jameson was complaining.

A short time later, Ruby had made her grand entrance as the Queen of Hearts, looking ravishing as always. It would fair to say, however, that what truly grabbed the attention of those already in attendance was that her King Consort was none other than Officer Ford – apparently Ruby had succeeded in her conquest.

"Hi Brad, thanks for coming," welcomed Jameson.

"When did this start?" whispered Jameson, when Brad went to the kitchen for a drink.

"A month ago, but I just wanted to keep him all to myself for a bit," said Ruby, with a saucy wink.

Connor and Didier arrived soon afterwards, looking adorable and quite huggable, as the Cheshire Cat and the Caterpillar. They had managed to find onesies of the characters, which looked amazing but were undoubtedly going to get uncomfortably hot as the evening wore on.

Nevertheless, it was the appearance of Nicolas' fellow models that caused the most ruckus of the evening. The magnificent men – along with their various boyfriends and fuck buddies – had come together to form the entire suit of hearts playing card guards. Each lad was wearing a cardboard panel, inscribed with their designated number, coupled with white sneakers and knee-high white socks with red piping. Underneath, however, all they were wearing was skimpy red speedos – from the latest CocKed range of course. They made quite the sight.

Ruby claimed them straight away, as was her right, although none of the group particularly seemed to mind, happy to play along for the evening. The fact that their king was a strapping specimen of manhood probably didn't hurt matters.

The townhouse soon filled with an assortment of familiar characters, although there was a bit of doubling up with two more Alices – both drag queens – plus a few more Cats and Hatters. Everyone got into the spirit of the evening, more so later in the evening after great qualities of alcohol had been consumed. Ruby was heard commanding decapitations left, right and center, while people held impromptu tea parties or played croquet – Jameson and Nicolas had set up plastic flamingos in the backyard, ready to use as mallets. Jameson was pleased that the party was going so well.

As the evening wore on, there was quite a bit of fraternization between the guests. At one point, Jameson noticed Matt and Trent leading about half the playing card guards downstairs to their apartment. He also saw Ruby and Brad becoming rather friendly with Ali who had come as the Knave of Hearts, with hands and tongues roaming freely between them.

Where's that's going to lead I wonder?

Around three in the morning the party started to really wind down with a good many of the guests having departed. Jameson offered one of the guest bedrooms to Connor and

Didier, both of whom were very inebriated and in no state to drive. Indeed, their onesies were now unbuttoned fully and showing quite a lot of skin. The other guest bedroom was claimed soon after by Ruby, who seemed to be enjoying the attentive company of her King and Knave.

To those few remaining, Jameson supplied a great many pillows and blankets, to make the sofas as comfortable as they could. Jameson made sure that everyone was settled for the night and made to go up the stairs to join Nicolas in bed. As he passed the door down the basement apartment, he heard all manner of muffled moans and groans.

Glad the boys are having fun.

He climbed the stairs to the bedroom, slipped off his costume and climbed in beside his bunny boyfriend – Nicolas had left the ears on.

"You're too cute," said Jameson, smiling at his adorable amour.

"I know…can I eat your carrot?" asked Nicolas, with a suggestive smile.

"Well I wouldn't want my poor bunny to starve," said Jameson, eagerly embracing their naughty role-play.

"Fuck yeah!" came a muffled voice through the wall.

Both boys laughed. The Master bedroom was next door to one of the guest bedrooms and across the hall from the other. Despite the sturdy walls the sound had a tendency to carry easily.

"Yeah, they've been a bit noisy on both sides," said Nicolas. "But it's been kinda hot to listen."

Once Jameson listened properly he soon heard to the distant sounds of many passions.

"From what I can tell Ruby is having a ball of a time with Brad and Ali, although it seems the boys are not adverse to pleasuring each other as well as their Queen. Connor and Didier, on the other hand, sound like they're trying for a gold medal in fucking," said Nicolas, as if he was commenting in a nature documentary.

"Well if you can't beat them…" began Jameson, suddenly feeling rather competitive.

They soon became lost in each other's bodies, writhing around becoming sweatier as their passions took hold. After a while, the sounds of the others faded away and they soon made enough noise to put even the most vocal of porn stars to shame.

Following much pumping, pounding and penetration of each other's asses, Jameson took Nicolas' glistening member into his mouth and proceeded to milk it dry – desperate to have his lover's seed. Barely a minute later, Nicolas gasped loudly and Jameson greedily swallowed down the load. Jameson savored the salty-sweet taste of his creamy reward as it filled his mouth and slid down his throat. Jameson jerked himself furiously and reached his own climax mere moments later, his semen spraying over the sheets.

When they were finally spent, they lay exhausted, wrapped in one another's arms.

"Glad you moved in?" asked Jameson.

"Well I'm certainly fond of my landlord."

Nicolas turned to give Jameson another slow, loving kiss.

* * *

Late the following morning Jameson awoke to see a familiar pair of china blue eyes lovingly staring at him.

"What you looking at?" Jameson said sleepily.

"My beautiful boyfriend. You got a problem with that Mister?" asked Nicolas, with mock seriousness.

"Not at all. Come here handsome."

Jameson drew in Nicolas for a morning cuddle. Naturally, one thing lead to another and before too long their morning woods had been relieved of their salty sap.

Feeling sated they headed to the bathroom for a quick shower together before heading downstairs to inspect the damage. There were glasses and plates strewn about the place but no real mess as far as Jameson could see. Surprisingly, judging by the burble of conversation coming from the backyard, everybody who'd stayed over seemed to already up and about, so the loved-up pair went to join the leftover guests. There were about fifteen people in the garden looking in varied states of recovery.

"Who's up for a big greasy breakfast?" offered Jameson.

Everyone seemed keen. Connor and Nicolas offered to help him while Matt, Didier and Trent went inside to help clean up the remnants of the party.

Before too long the delicious fried smell of bacon and eggs wafted through the house. When it was all done Jameson and the boys set out the plates and had people eat buffet style off of paper plates, as there were too many people to sit around the table and it would help with the cleaning up later.

After they had devoured the tasty fare, Nicolas suggested a beach expedition seeing it was such a stunning sunny day.

Of those assembled only half expressed a desire to go to the beach with the others begging off and apparently preferring the comforting embrace of their homes instead. So, Jameson, Nicolas, Connor, Didier, Matt, Trent, Ruby, Brad and Ali piled into two cars, once they discerned who was actually fit to drive, and headed off for Murdoch Beach for some fun in the sun.

They soon arrived at the popular naturist beach, which was already quite crowded but they were luckily able to find a spot not too far from the lapping waves. As they all stripped off Jameson couldn't help sneaking a glance at Brad who revealed a veritable monster between his legs.

Lucky Ruby…and Ali too apparently!

A thought no doubt shared by all the boys in their group. The sun beat down on the tired revelers, helping to recharge their batteries and restore them to health.

As he lay on the towel next to his boyfriend soaking up the sun, Jameson couldn't believe how far he had come and how fortunate he was to have Nicolas in his life. A man who had helped heal a heart that he'd thought irrevocably broken into a million pieces.

Jameson had been to hell and back but from having known such dark despair he could appreciate the goodness in life even more, although he wasn't certain that he needed so steep a learning curve. Thankfully, his book was still selling and the sequel was in final editing at Hastings House, not that he thought he'd be an international bestseller…but you never know.

He also felt that he may even be open to the possibility of marriage again one day, the light in his heart that Nicolas had given him had made him feel that perhaps anything was possible. Jameson turned on his side and leant forward to stroke Nicolas' face.

"All good?" asked Nicolas, with a warm smile.

"Never been better," replied Jameson, as he leant forward and gave Nicolas the gentlest of kisses.

ABOUT THE AUTHOR

Jimi could be considered to be something of a refined blend of Australian/Polish heritage – given his passion for the arts, vodka and BBQs. He now lives in Paris with his wonderfully understanding French husband and cats.

For other of his raunchy ramblings and published work, feel free to browse http://www.jimify.me follow him on Twitter & Instagram @jimifyme or show your devotion at facebook.com/JIMIFY.ME

OTHER DIGITAL TITLES BY JIMI GONINAN

For all Jimi's titles please visit his page at lydianpress.com

IN PRINT FROM LYDIAN PRESS

DOM'S DELIGHTS

Come on in and taste the love!

Dom has worked hard pursuing his dreams of delighting the masses with his tasty treats - indeed his cream has been eagerly eaten all about the town. Now he has almost everything he ever dreamed of – a successful business, loving friends and a beautiful beau. There's just one more thing he needs to make his life complete...to finally marry the man of his dreams!

There's so much to do before the big day but luckily, they encounter more than a few friendly helping hands along the way. Follow the adventures of Dom and his merry band of lusty lads as they help him overcome pesky obstacles and prepare for the most important day of his life. Everyone deserves a good old-fashioned happy ending, after all.

Lydian Press is dedicated to bringing you the finest GLBTQ erotic literature on the web.

Visit us on the web at:

http://lydianpress.com